DEATH'S KISS

DEATH'S KISS

LEXI SWANN

This one is for my sisters.
Always forge your own path.

CHAPTER ONE

THE EVERLASTING WAIT

MONTHS. SHE'D WAITED MONTHS FOR BRENT'S return, eager to begin their life together once the last of the dark sorcerers had been wiped from their lands. A brutal group of wronged women who had declared war on their vast continent, causing a war that had been fought by the King's men for the past several years as they scoured the land for the witches. The war had already turned once bountiful fields of crops into a colossal wasteland, which would take decades, if not centuries, to ever become useful again. And the war had taken countless men from their families, including her Brent.

She didn't think his absence would affect her as much as it

had. She thought she had become comfortable with her loneliness. She'd always been somewhat of a hermit, or so the other townsfolk had whispered as she'd pass them by on the cobblestone streets of Dargonia. When she'd met Brent though, everything in her world seemed to change.

She could hardly remember the feel of his rough, slightly calloused hand as it caressed her soft, delicate skin. The way his nose always pressed into the side of hers as his lips captured hers as if he needed her kiss more than the air they breathed. How he always seemed to smell spicy and sweet all at once, a hint of citrus orange beneath his manly scent. And how his dazzling sapphire eyes regarded her as if she were the only woman worth seeing.

Sighing, she stood from where she sat by the window, gazing through the clear glass at the fields surrounding her home as she held onto an old fashioned, worn pocket watch. She supposed she should head into town again, see if the townspeople had heard anything of the soldiers and when they may return. It had been weeks since she'd heard rumors of dark sorcery; so long ago that she had begun to expect Brent back days before now. It had been disappointing when he hadn't ambled up her front stoop.

She grabbed her coin purse, in case she decided to purchase something from the market, and hid it within the folds of her lemon-yellow skirts before stowing the pocket watch away in the drawer she kept her purse within. Once she had shrugged into her chocolate brown, leather jacket and buttoned a few of the buttons, she grabbed a ribbon from the jar by the door and left her home. She had her hair tied in a loose ponytail before her feet touched the dirt path leading to her front porch.

It was a beautiful day, though no matter how warm the sun's rays felt on her face, she couldn't bring herself to find any happiness. Not until her lover returned and wed her as he'd promised. Only then would she allow herself to feel anything other than the gnawing dread that something bad had happened. She didn't know how she knew, but she feared the worst regardless. Hoping it to be just displaced worry, she had continued her wait as the weeks had grown into months.

Fall fast approached their lands as the breeze blowing through the trees became colder everyday. The sun still shone brightly, and the greenery had yet to begin its shedding of colors. She had to believe that the king would let his men return before winter settled into their land, freezing all who dared stay out too long. Even he must have a way to communicate with the men protecting them, who'd given their vows to hunt the sorcerers and end the threat to their people. Yet, if he could reach them, he'd not thought it wise to share news of their warriors with his people. Crystal's patience had begun to wear thin.

The horses within her stables could be heard several feet away as she approached. She kept two, one of which belonged solely to her while the other had been kept should she have a guest requiring a steed. Of course, she'd ride them both often enough just to keep them trained proper. Today, however, she preferred to saddle Dawn, her own Dargosian bred horse.

The door creaked as she opened it and stepped inside the stables. She'd spent the morning in here cleaning stalls, and she'd spend the evening here as well when she came back to brush the horses down and ready them for the night. The two large beasts nickered as she came up to their gates, and she took a moment to rub each of their noses, cooing terms of endearment as she did. Moments later, she had Dawn ready and she swung up into the saddle in one smooth motion before trotting down the dirt path toward town.

Shortly after an hour later, she pulled on the reins to slow Dawn down to a slow walk. She headed straight to the tavern, where a railing sat on the other side of a trough of water. She hopped off the horse, tied the reins to the railing, and walked toward the entrance after patting Dawn's side affectionately. Water sloshed from the trough as Crystal pushed through the swinging doors and entered a nearly vacant tavern, which wasn't surprising this time of day.

As always, the room smelled of piss, cigarette smoke, alcohol, and sex. With her nose wrinkled, she marched toward the barkeep. She didn't bother sitting. She wouldn't be staying long.

The barkeep grinned at her as she placed her hands on the counter between them. He had to be missing at least three of his teeth from what she could see. She surmised nothing but alcohol, women, and peanuts would do that to a man. His missing teeth wouldn't be such a problem if they had been the only thing rough about him. Try as she might, she couldn't even pretend to succumb to his charms to get the information she desired. Brutal honesty it would have to be then.

"Lookin' for work, my lady? A figure like that would fetch some fine coins around here," he asked as he wriggled his brows as if to add, 'if you know what I mean.'

Oh, she knew what he meant, but interest couldn't have been further from her intentions.

"I'm afraid I have plenty of work. I'm actually here to see if you've heard any information about the king's army?" she questioned. Her fingers had already become sticky from the dirty counter, and she lifted her hands to wipe them on her skirts. With the lack of patrons around here, washing his counters and tidying this place up were the least he could do.

"What news are ya seekin'?" He busied himself by pouring himself a mug of ale.

"I wish to know when they're expected to return."

"You mean you haven't heard yet?"

"Heard what?"

"They returned three days ago, my lady. They brought news of their success, and the king, being so pleased, has decided to throw a celebration for the lands in two weeks' time." He regarded her with dark eyes that had grown skeptical.

"They've returned? All of them? Are you sure?" She ignored the look he gave her. There was no room for it as her worry seemed to become a tangible thing between them.

"What, lass? Do ya live under a rock? Yes! All of them!

Well," he paused and chewed on his lip, "that is... the ones who'd survived the battles, which I do hear were quite fierce and gruesome."

She turned from him then. The rest of his words lost in the buzzing of her crowded mind. It was as if the entire world's cicadas had thrown a concert within her eardrums. Her vision narrowed, and the air became terribly thin. She crossed the dirty bar toward the exit. She needed air.

The men had returned. They'd returned days ago while she'd been sat at her window watching and waiting as she did her needlepoint. Where was Brent?

"Are you okay, my lady?" the barkeep asked, but she didn't hear his concern as she half-fell, half-walked through the swinging doors, out onto the front veranda, and down the wooden steps toward Dawn.

She leaned on her horse while she gulped for air, pressing her forehead into the blond mane of her steed while she concentrated on breathing.

She needed to request an audience with her king to hear of news of Brent. There must have been some reason why he hadn't returned to her when the soldiers had come home. She couldn't begin to think of those reasons though, not until she knew for certain what had transpired. Because if she did begin to let her mind wander, it would travel nowhere good, and her heart couldn't handle that. So instead, she loosened the reins around the railing and mounted Dawn.

It seemed she was off to see her king.

CHAPTER TWO

THE DARKEST DAY

DAWN'S SLOW WALK THROUGH THE STREETS kept A steady rhythm in the air around them as they made their way through town. The castle sat near the rear walls, where every window along the back of the structure faced the tall snow-capped mountains in the distance. A large lake sat not far from the rear walls, and Crystal knew from experience how the sun danced across the top of the water and cast the mountains and surrounding greenery in an almost magical light.

Her work as a seamstress had brought her to the servants' quarters of the palace a few times, and each trip there had taken her down a corridor with a glass wall that stretched the length, highlighting the beauty of the land in which they lived.

She hadn't been hired on as staff at the palace, not for a lack of the castle staff trying either, but her mother had been, when she had still lived. In fact, from the stories she heard and from what little she could remember, Crystal knew her mother had been the head seamstress at the castle. Crystal had always thought that the staff offered her small jobs from time to time as a way to check in on her for her mother's sake, and she didn't mind their small courtesies, she just didn't want to be part of the game. After all, that's all court life was.

Her mother had loved the game. She would gossip with the other seamstresses as they worked, and she had a way of knowing all the juicy details regarding the ladies and lords. Her work was always highly valued, and her position on staff was secured for as ever long as she wished. Nearly everyone within the palace would request her work, but what Crystal had loved most about her mother was the fact that she had never stuck her nose out of joint. She was the seamstress of royalty, but even the bog lady could count on Crystal's mother for repairs or new purchases.

The townsfolk stayed out of Crystal's way for the most part as she trekked toward the gates barring her from their king. They usually didn't cause her many issues, only speaking to her on occasions they required her services and, even then, they only hired her if the seamstress in town had been overbooked.

For the most part, she enjoyed the peace. In times like now, however, she knew she'd have heard news of the army's return sooner if she had had a friend in town to share the news with her. The seamstresses who had known her mother didn't often set foot outside the city, so she couldn't fault them for not bringing her news. She had chosen a solitary life, and so a solitary life she lived. Nothing could be done about that now, though.

Glancing around the dirt paths, she noticed several men from the army milling about with their families. She hadn't recognized them on her way into town, but she supposed her heart couldn't believe they had returned without Brent having shown up on her stoop like he'd promised so many moons ago.

There, just in front of a merchant's stall of fruits, stood Borris, one of the soldiers she'd often seen with Brent. He had his children tugging at the uniform he still wore, and his wife placed apples into a sack next to him, his hand never leaving the small of her back. Crystal would have gone to speak with him regarding Brent, but she didn't want to interrupt him when he'd just returned to his family after being away for months.

Instead, she hopped off her horse and led her to the railings outside the gates. With Dawn tethered to the railings and feasting on some bright green grass, Crystal made her way to the gates and stopped before them. It wasn't long before two men with great swords strapped to their backs greeted her from the other side.

"State your business," one of the men said, his voice gruffer than a grizzly's.

The man who spoke approached the gate barring her

entrance. He wore the uniform of the king's guard; navy cargo-style pants with a matching button up shirt beneath a jacket. Along with his great sword, a small crossbow sat hanging at his waist. His hair was black as night, and his eyes a piercing green as he stared through the bars with a creased brow, waiting for her to reply. He knew exactly who she was, but the king's guard were sticklers for following policy.

Crystal straightened her back and adjusted her yellow skirts. After licking her lips and meeting his gaze, she spoke. "I wish to seek an audience with the king."

"What for?" the other guard asked, his head tilting to the side. His features were a complete contrast to the other man. Where the first guard had dark hair and glittering green eyes and a deep voice, this man's hair was whitish blond, his eyes a deep shade of brown, and his voice almost nasally.

"I seek news of the army. I see several of the soldiers have returned, but my beau has yet to join my side," she replied, twisting the ends of her chestnut-hued ponytail nervously. It was possible they wouldn't grant her request and she'd have to return home empty handed, or empty hearted, depending on how she looked at it.

The guards looked at one another for a moment. Apparently, they knew each other well enough to pass conversations with their gazes. Crystal remained where she stood, waiting for them to finish their silent discussion. With a shrug, the gruff-voiced guard stepped forward and slid the locks open before swinging the ebony painted bars outward.

She sidestepped the iron bars and made her way into the courtyard. Once the gate had clattered closed again, the gruff guard began to lead the way into the castle.

A servant stood stationed inside the two story, arched, azure hued front doors, waiting to serve. The room itself looked magnificent, as always. She had always adored the show of elegance as soon as you stepped foot within the castle's walls. Regal red carpets lined the pathways to the hallways, over glistening marble tiles. The walls had been painted a rich gold and beautiful tapestries hung every few feet along them, depicting various historical moments. Her eyes flicked to the newest tapestry hanging, already the wars against the dark sorcerers was put into needlework and held on display along the walls of the great room.

She paused for a moment, admiring the tapestries she knew to have been made by her mother. The crowning of King Edgar Barnes was her favorite, with all the rich colors and detail put into it. He stood upon his throne, a smile sent his wife's way, who stood just off to the side, as a crown was placed atop his head. It was her mother's favorite, which was precisely why she favored it as well.

"Henry, take this woman to Madge and let her know that the lady requests an audience with the king," the guard spoke, and with a nod from the servant—Henry—he turned on his heel and left.

Henry appeared to be in his late thirties, but she didn't know his age exactly. The lines of his jaw were prominent, squared, and clean shaven. He wore the uniform of a member of the palace staff; dark trousers, crisply ironed, and a white dress shirt under a black jacket with the dragon spewing fire emblem of their land. When he stood at attention, as he had been when they'd first entered, his hands remained clasped firmly behind his back, almost as if he were a statue.

He gave her a quick look up and down before motioning in a circular movement of his wrist for her to, "Come right this way, miss." It didn't matter how often she visited the palace, he had never dropped the formalities, and she doubted if he ever would.

She hadn't expected to be taken to see the king when she'd left her home this morning, and now as she followed Henry's back down the corridors, embarrassment flared to life within her. She should have worn something more appropriate than her current attire, which consisted of a bright, simple yellow dress beneath her small chocolate hued leather jacket, all of which had a layer of dust coating it from her hours on horseback that day. If her mother could see her now, she'd be mortified.

After walking down hallway after hallway and taking so many twists and turns, Crystal was lost. She had never been in this part of the palace. She was thankful for her guide as they turned yet another corner and stopped before an open doorway. Henry stopped so quickly, she almost waltzed right into his back.

"Remain here, if you will," he said, his speech cultured into what best suited the royals he served.

Crystal nodded and waited as he entered the room and approached another woman who sat behind a large oak desk. After a moment of hushed speech, the two of them made their way out of the room and stood before Crystal. The lady, whom she knew to be Madge, had hair the color of snow, weathered brown eyes, and a look of annoyance creased between her brows. Her white hair had been pulled into a pristine bun, and her attire matched that of the male servant, except hers was a dress and apron.

"Henry says you wish to speak to the king?" Madge asked with a raised brow.

"I do."

Madge glanced at Henry. "I've got it from here, Henry," she dismissed, and then waited in silence for Henry to leave as she stared at Crystal.

Her no-nonsense stare began to make Crystal uncomfortable as she shifted her weight from foot to foot while Henry's footsteps sounded quieter and quieter as he left them alone. Once he turned a corner out of sight, Madge looked Crystal up and down, sizing her up.

"Will you take me to see the king?" Crystal asked timidly. Her voice sounded weak even to her ears, and she inwardly cringed at how nervous a servant managed to make her feel. If Brent could see her now, he'd be ashamed of her, she thought to herself sadly.

"I suppose," Madge replied, pulling a wrinkled kerchief

from her apron pocket and wiping her hands, though Crystal could see no grime covering her leathery skin. "Follow me, child."

They walked through the castle for several minutes, down hallways filled with closed doors, up twisted marble steps, and past several lounges and other fine rooms fully decorated to suit a king's wealth. Crystal watched in amazement as they made their way through the castle, looking at things she'd never seen before on her previous visits. They traveled areas she'd never walked before, and her gaze greedily took in the sights and wonder. Oh, to live like royalty, she mused.

They had maintained some small talk as they'd made their way through the palace. Madge asked how Crystal had been, wondering why they hardly saw her around anymore. Crystal explained how she'd been more focused on maintaining her cozy home out on the countryside, growing a few small gardens and keeping her horses well looked after.

The conversation darkened slightly when Madge asked the obvious question. Why was Crystal seeking an audience with the king? So, she told her everything. Madge had been one of her mother's closest friends. If there was anyone she could trust, it was Madge. The only reason Crystal didn't seek out her counsel more often was the fact that being head of a palace's staff took up more hours than there were in a day. She didn't want to be a bother to an already over-worked woman.

When Madge came to a halt, Crystal nearly ran into her. People really had to stop doing that, one of these times she wasn't going to halt in time. Oblivious to her plight, Madge swept her arm and gesticulated for her to enter the open doorway at which they'd stopped. Shelves, from floor to ceiling, made up each wall; they even lined the lone bay window, which provided the perfect reading nook with its fluffy purple and silver cushions. Books filled in every space along each shelf, and a ladder rested along every wall, should a reader wish to reach the upper most shelves of books.

She made her way into the room, her eyes wide as she stared at the walls in wonder. She barely noticed the large, clunky looking wooden desk sat diagonally in the front corner, or the pristine white, large cushion sofa and chair positioned before a roaring fire in an elegantly designed fireplace. She had a few bookcases at home filled with novels that had been double parked on the shelves, but her own meager collection couldn't be compared to this.

Madge cleared her throat and Crystal glanced up, noticing Madge hadn't even entered the room yet. When their eyes met, Madge said, "If you wouldn't mind waiting here, I'll see that the king knows you wish to speak to him. Pick a book, dear. The king will make time when he sees fit. You know how it is." Then she dipped her chin and left Crystal alone to admire the wonders surrounding her. She could wait days in this room and never get bored. Not knowing how long it would take the king to see her, she meandered toward the shelves and began reading the spines.

CHAPTER THREE

THE BROKEN HEART

LOSING TRACK OF TIME BECAME EASIER WHEN books were involved. Crystal had learned that lesson at an early age. However, having learned that lesson ages ago still didn't prevent her embarrassment when the king entered. She'd never dream of greeting the king in such a manner as she managed today, but as her wait for Madge's return had stretched longer and longer, Crystal's curiosity grew larger and larger. Before she knew what she was doing, her fingers had gripped the spine of a book she hadn't read before, a book about slaying dragons, and she opened it with her eyes wide with excitement.

When the king coughed to garner her attention, she jumped

from where she'd been lying on the soft sofa, nearly dropping the book she'd been reading as she did. Heat rushed to her cheeks as she straightened her skirts with one hand, her other still holding onto the novel firmly.

"I apologize, Your Majesty!" she cried out, embarrassed.

In all of her visits to the castle, not once had she ever come face to face with the king. At least, not in such an intimate manner. She'd seen him seated upon the throne when he listened to what his people needed or wanted, but she'd never been in a room alone with him. Sure, he probably had his guards stationed just outside the door, but that wasn't the point.

He looked at her, a slight lift to his lip the only sign of his amusement, but his amusement only furthered her embarrassment.

She didn't know how he wasn't overheating beneath the regal robes; the royal purple fabric fluffed upward so high that his shoulders appeared to reach the bottoms of his ears, and they fell to the floor in a cape-like cloak fashion. The crown glittered atop his head, where it sat in a mess of golden-brown curls. He was a handsome man who would have no issue finding someone to spend his life with even if he wasn't the king, but he'd vowed long ago, after the loss of his queen, never to take comfort in another woman's bosom. As far as Crystal had heard, it was a vow he had kept.

His lime green eyes sparked as his lips tugged upward. He waved a hand, his fingers riddled with gemstones and jewels, as he entered what she'd begun referring to as the library. He approached where she stood, before the crisp white sofa, until he came next to the matching chair. He dipped his chin as if to say, 'after you,' and when she slowly sat down, unsure if that was the proper protocol or not, he moved to follow, sitting in the chair at her side.

They turned in their seats until they faced each other, and as a tiny woman, dressed in the same uniform Madge had worn, entered the room with a tray containing tea and sugar cookies, the pair waited in silence while the servant placed down the offering. Once she had left the room, the king bent forward and poured himself some tea, and then he held the tiny pot out to her with his bushy brow raised. She shook her head no in response and waited for him to sit back in his chair. She figured it best to let him begin the conversation; he was the king after all.

"Now what brings a young lady such as yourself to seek an audience with me?" he questioned, watching her from above the rim of his china cup as he sipped his tea. Steam rose in a tendril dance, and the sweet scent filled the room.

"I'd been hoping you could better tell me what had happened with the army, Your Majesty," she replied, her voice low, unsure of herself now that she sat before the king. It had seemed a fine idea to seek him out for answers, right up until this moment. She chastised herself silently for her cowardice; Brent deserved her strength now. Who knew what danger might have befallen her love.

The king took another small sip of his drink before he

leaned forward and placed the cup down on the coffee table. He grabbed a sugar cookie from the tray and offered it to her. She politely declined. She hadn't come for tea and cookies; she'd come for answers.

"Do you not live in town, my lady? I thought all the townsfolk had heard by now. The army has returned victorious and we'll be holding a celebration in a few days' time."

"But not all of them have returned..."

"No, of course not, my lady. There's often much loss when such fierce battles take place." The king dusted his sugar-coated fingers on the velvety material of his robes. His face had fallen as he spoke of the loss of his men, and Crystal almost felt bad for pushing the subject further.

"I've been waiting in my home, out on the countryside hills, for my love to return to me. You wouldn't happen to know anything about what might have happened to him, would you? His name is Brent Maverson."

She couldn't read his face, and as she waited for his response, she couldn't help but feel the pit of her stomach twist and churn. She needed to know what had happened. Needed to know if she should expect a wounded soldier to return to her, or if the unthinkable had occurred. She chewed her bottom lip as she waited, wringing her hands in her lap.

"I'm sorry, my lady. I'm afraid I don't. You can check the sick house if you wish. The men who were wounded have all made it to our healers by now. If you can't find him there, you have my deepest condolences. I know the pain of losing your love. It's a pain I wish I could eradicate from our lands as easily as we defeated the dark sorcerers. I pray you find your lad in the sick house," the king said. Sadness hung over every feature of his face, his green eyes almost dimming with the painful memories of his own haunted loss. He spoke from the heart.

Crystal rose to her feet, blinking back tears at the emotion she felt lifting from the king. She looked away and wiped her face dry. When she looked back toward the king, she said, "Thank you for your time, Your Majesty. I apologize again for touching your things. Here." She held the book out to him.

He held up a hand. "No, it's okay, my lady. You keep it. I hope you find who you're seeking in the sick house. Please, if you require anything else, just send word. I promised the late queen I'd look after our people, and I intend to keep my last promise to her."

"Of course, Your Majesty. Thank you again, sir," she replied, curtsying as best she could.

As she left the room, she found Madge standing just outside the doorway in wait. Without a word between them, Madge showed Crystal out of the palace with a solemn silence that spoke volumes. Madge had heard what had passed between her and the king, and now she knew of Crystal's loss.

Crystal held the gifted book to her chest like a shield, knowing the next place she traversed would give her the answers she sought, whether they were the answers she wanted or not.

The sick house was only a short walk from where the castle sat, so Crystal didn't bother with mounting Dawn. After untying the reins, she walked her horse down the dirt paths, holding her book to her chest, toward the building she feared would break her heart. She needed to know what had become of Brent. She wouldn't be able to rest otherwise.

The local townsfolk moved out of her way as she passed, and the further into town she traversed, the more she recognized the men from the king's army. She couldn't believe how she had missed them on her way into town, but as she watched more and more of them with their wives and children, the weight in her stomach grew heavier and heavier.

Brent should be with her right now, loving her. It had been so long since she'd last felt his arms wrapped around her, since his gentle touch as he dragged his calloused fingers over her bare skin had caused her to shiver with need. The mere thought of him, of them together, filled her with such heat that she had to pause her walking to slow her rapidly beating heart.

Dawn's nose swung sideways, curious as to what had halted them. Crystal took that moment to tuck the book the king had caught her reading into one of the saddlebags, and then she used her free hand to rub Dawn's pale beige face lovingly, bringing her lips to the side of her nose for a chaste kiss.

"Let's get this over with, shall we?" Crystal said quietly

before leading the horse through town toward the sick house.

The sick house was a long wooden cabin in the shape of a rectangle. It had more windows than most any other building in town, and the vast majority of them were open to allow the cool breeze to air out the rooms inside. Along the front lawn of the establishment sat a vibrant garden filled with various flowers, of which Crystal could name only a few, with a few benches overlooking the beauty. On one such bench sat a man whose back hunched forward at what had to have been a painful angle. He appeared to be missing the lower half of his right leg, and a male nursemaid stood not far away, ready to aid the man back inside once he'd had his fill of fresh air.

After tying Dawn to a post under a large tree next to the path leading toward the sick house, Crystal made her way up the walkway and into the wood building. As soon as she stepped inside, the noise of the sick house made her heart ache as she cringed at the sounds. Cries rang out from various rooms; some deep manly voices, some piercing womanly voices, and others wrenched themselves from wailing children. Every sound hurt her soul, and she began fearing the worst had happened to her Brent.

A small desk sat next to the door, with a young attendant waiting to direct any newcomers. Crystal stepped forward and waited for the woman to notice her. A few seconds later, she glanced up from the papers she'd been scribbling furiously on and smiled at Crystal. She wore a cap over her head, the strings of which held it firmly in place, tied beneath her chin, and effectively ensured her dark red hair wouldn't interfere with her work on patients; every nursemaid wore something similar atop their heads.

"Are you ill, or visiting?" the woman asked, her eyes darting up and down Crystal as if she were attempting to answer her own question.

"I'm not sure. I was wondering if you'd be able to tell me if a certain soldier arrived here after the battles?" Crystal asked, shifting her weight from foot to foot.

"Possibly. Though, I should warn you, some wounded have come back badly injured and without any form of identifying them."

Crystal gasped, her hand lifting to her mouth. She closed her mouth and breathed deeply through her nose, lifting her head to the ceiling above as she settled herself down again. Even if she gave this woman her love's name, there was a possibility she wouldn't know what had happened to him for sure until she checked each room with an unidentified wounded man inside. She didn't know if her heart could take much more.

After she regained her composure, she dipped her head and asked, "Would you happen to know if you have a Brent Maverson here?"

The attendant flipped through the folders contained on her desk until she found what she'd been looking for, and then her finger dragged down the page as she silently read a list of names to herself. There were three such pages for her to scan, and when she finished, the look on her face told Crystal the search had been in vain.

"How many unidentified soldiers do you have here?" Crystal asked, chewing her lip at the thought of what she was about to request.

The woman scanned the page again. "It looks like we have six."

"Would it be possible for me to check these soldiers to see if one of them is my Brent?"

A sad look crossed the woman's blue eyes, but she nodded her consent before she stood. "I'll show you the way."

They made their way through the entrance, which had a small area for the nursemaids to perform their initial exam should any new patients enter the sick house. From the main entrance, several hallways branched off in a few different directions, one of which led to a stairwell upward. They climbed the stairs, the sounds of pain and horror rising as they reached the second floor, and they walked past a few closed doors before they stopped outside of one.

"I should warn you, ma'am. They were unidentifiable and barely alive when they were brought to us. Odds are they won't survive their injuries. Should your Brent be in one of these rooms I'm taking you to, your only option may be to sit by his side for his final days." The attendant waited for a moment and so Crystal nodded her understanding.

Then the woman opened the door and stepped out of Crystal's way. The smell that came from the room made her choke, and she turned her head to cough in the sleeve of her jacket as she covered her nose.

Burnt flesh. Nothing quite smelled like it. She'd never come across the scent before, but she'd never forget how it brought tears to her eyes with how foul it smelled. She took a deep breath from within the crook of her elbow, dropped her arm to her side, and then timidly stepped into the room.

Dust motes danced on the few rays peeking through the sheer curtains, the heavier drapes had been pushed to the side to allow what little sunlight was left in the day to flow through the room. A sick bed sat nestled in the corner of the room, within the shadows where the sun couldn't reach. No candles burned inside the room, but smoke wafted from one next to the bedside, as if the wounded man within the bed had blown it out as the door to his room swung open. Shame, the emotion hung heavy in the room and Crystal knew it came from the poor soul she approached.

"Sir," Crystal's voice cut through the room, sounding loud to her ears. She lowered her tone. "I'm searching for my love. He hasn't returned to me from the battles."

Her footsteps brought her closer, the stench of his burnt flesh stinging her eyes. She bit her lip to avoid making a foul face, she didn't want to give this man more reasons to feel ashamed.

As she came next to the bed, she could make out more of the man with such massive injuries. His face looked away, toward the wall, but the skin of his back, arms, and parts of his scalp that she could glimpse from the low light in the room were covered in dark crusts of burned flesh. The flames had melted hair to his head, wrinkling the skin in a pattern of pain and suffering she couldn't imagine.

"Would you please let me see if you're the man I've been waiting for?" she asked timidly.

She was afraid he would be who she had been searching for, but she was also afraid he wasn't. Her mixed emotions had her so confused, she wasn't even sure which fear overcame the other, and as she watched the man before her let out a strangled sigh, she knew she was just afraid altogether.

Slowly, as if every minuscule movement he made sent overwhelming pain through his body, the man twisted his head to peer up at his visitor. The pillow beneath his head seemed discolored, darker than the crisp edges of the pillowcase, and she figured it to be caused by blood or flakes of burnt flesh tearing away. The burns covered seventy-five percent of his face, leaving only part of his left cheek and lips unscathed. It hid his identity from his comrades, but it left enough untouched that she knew this man wasn't her Brent. She'd know his eyes and lips anywhere. No, these weren't the lips that had tickled her earlobe while his fingers had tangled in her dark locks of hair.

Her shoulders slumped, and the man's face darkened with his own emotions of being let down. He'd been hoping she'd claim him, she realized. The nursemaid's words came back to her then, about how the men who had come to them unidentifiable were injured beyond repair and were most likely awaiting their deaths. These dark rooms would depress even the lightest of souls. What a horrible way to leave this land after the heroics they had fought for their people.

Crystal placed a gentle hand to the man's chest, where a patch of bandages covered his wounds. She didn't use any pressure in her touch, she merely wished him to see she was not afraid of the way he appeared. She dropped to her knee, bringing her face level to his. And as the confusion darted across his brow, she spoke.

"You are not the man I've been waiting for, but you have my utmost gratitude for your service. I promise I will be back once I've finished my search, if that would please you, of course."

She fixed him with a stare as she waited for a response. A lightness seemed to fill his gaze, and the left side of his mouth lifted in an almost imperceptible smile. He didn't speak a word, but he let his eyes drift closed, and as he nodded his consent, a tear fell from the corner of his eye.

"I'll be back soon," she said, rising to her feet.

After she left his room, she took a deep breath before nodding to the nursemaid to continue showing her the rooms. Every room held similar patients. All from the army, all unclaimed, and all without hope. She gave every single one of them her word that she'd return.

None of the rooms held Brent, and her search for her love had come to a brutal end. She hadn't found him, but in not finding him she'd figured out what had happened to him.

Brent had died as a soldier in the king's army, and a piece of her had died with him.

CHAPTER FOUR

THE BEGINNINGS OF A PLAN

THE ANTICIPATION GREW UNTIL CRYSTAL'S NEED became overwhelming as Brent entered her bedroom. She lifted her head from her pillows, the thin strap of her sheer white sleeping gown slipping down her shoulder as she peered across her room at the man who had stolen her heart. He took a few, slow steps toward where she lay, his fingers working the buttons of his fatigues as his lips twisted into a seductive grin that had her pulse racing. She watched as he revealed more and more of his chest, his movements almost agonizingly slow.

She'd waited for this moment for months. She needed to feel the heat of his skin beneath her palms, the depth of his kiss upon her tongue, and the length of him between her thighs. She sat up as the tip of her tongue darted across her bottom lip, her mouth suddenly dry with anticipation, and as Brent's fingers finally reached the last button, she could take no more and leaped from the bed.

Ripping the shirt from his shoulders, she pulled him toward her as she walked backward until her legs hit the edge of her large bed. She lay down, pulling him down to her with her grip around the back of his neck. Lifting her head, she brought her impatient lips to meet his, and she relished the heat that built as his tongue darted between her lips, tasting her just as she had needed to taste him.

"I've missed you," she whispered, trailing kisses from his lips to his neck.

The calloused skin of his hands tickled her as he pushed the remaining strap from her shoulder and pulled the material down, down, down. Her head tilted backward as her heart raced with each subtle touch he gave, and she never wanted this feeling of euphoria to end. His heated lips kissed the flat of her stomach as his hands roamed up her body, the pads of his thumb teasing her as he nearly passed them over her breasts. Her breathing came ragged as she basked in the attention he gave her.

She needed to feel his skin against hers. She brought her hands down his back until the waist of his pants, and then she followed the hem to the button and began pulling at the opening frantically. She felt his smile through the kisses he trailed up her stomach, the soft whiskers from his five o'clock shadow itching as he kissed between her breasts. She pushed his pants down as far as she could from the angle she lay, and then reached for his head and pulled him up for a kiss.

"I need you, and I need you now," she told him.

She twisted on the mattress, wanting to trade places with him, but as she flipped herself over, he was suddenly gone. She glanced around the room for a frantic moment, wondering what had happened to him. The bedroom door hadn't been opened though, and as she realized that, she remembered the events of the previous day as a lonely tear slid down her cheek.

She must have dreamed the entire thing, she realized. Brent would never come home to her again. He had never made his way home from the battles he'd fought for the king. He hadn't been wounded in the sick house. No, Crystal knew the worst had happened and death had claimed her love too soon. She flipped back over and rubbed the sleep from her eyes.

The rapid beat of her heart let her know the dream had affected her in more ways than one. She ached for Brent's touch still, but that touch would never come.

Climbing out of bed, Crystal went to the window to see if she could gauge what time it was. Was there any point in heading back to bed? Or should she just start her day now? The sky above was still dark as night, but on the horizon, she could already see the shades of blue were lightening into shades of almost pink. There was no point in going back to bed.

She made her way to her kitchen, readjusting the sleeves of

her sleeping gown as she walked down the hallway. Her home wasn't too large, but it would have made a fine home for her and Brent.

When she entered the kitchen, her feet took her to the cupboard that housed the coffee mugs on instinct, and after she took down her favorite cup, she proceeded to brew herself half a pot of coffee. She felt as though she were half-awake, half-dazed until the heavy scent of caffeine filled the air.

With her coffee in hand, Crystal went into the living room. She pulled the book the king had gifted her from the bookshelf and made herself comfortable in the reading chair by the window. She knew Brent wouldn't be finding his way home, but she'd become accustomed to reading by the front window every morning, nonetheless.

After she finished her coffee, and a few chapters, Crystal decided to keep her promises. She placed the book back on the shelf until the next morning and washed the cup she'd used, and then she headed outside, where the sun could finally be seen in the distance as it made its climb into the clear blue sky. A garden stretched across the front of the house, and although she wouldn't consider herself as having a green thumb per se, she enjoyed the colors blooming out front her windows and how, if the breeze was right, the floral scent would drift into her open windows on a nice, hot day. She didn't know the kinds of flowers housed within her gardens; she only picked them based on their petals and beauty. She'd trusted the woman at the market to tell her which would be easily maintained, and she hadn't had any issues with her garden yet.

If Crystal planned to see the wounded soldiers again today, she did not want to arrive empty handed. She knelt in front of her gardens with her pruning shears and trailed her fingers gently through the various petals. As she cut several stems, gathering the most vibrant of her collection, she remembered the men who had fought for their land but now lay alone, possibly dying while the people they'd fought for hadn't a clue. They were heroes. They deserved so much more than what they were currently receiving.

Finished her task, she brought her fistful of flowers into the house and set them on the kitchen table. Once she had her pruning shears back in the drawer where they belonged, she washed her hands and headed upstairs to shower and change out of her night gown. She enjoyed living so far away from everyone else, having her privacy after the childhood she'd had meant the world to her.

A short ten minutes later, she smelled of lavender and her night gown had been replaced by a simple navy-blue dress with three-quarter length sleeves and a skirt that hugged her slight curves to just above the knee. Donning her ankle-high, black leather boots, she grabbed her jacket and the flowers, and went to saddle up Dawn.

She headed to town after giving both horses the attention they deserved, rubbing them down, refilling their water troughs, and ensuring they had enough hay and oats for the day, and after Dawn had nibbled on some breakfast, they left the stables for town.

The mid-morning sun dried the dew drops on the grass and warmed the land to the point Crystal nearly wanted to remove her jacket. She didn't want to arrive at the sick house sweaty and unladylike. Besides, she still needed to pick up something else before she made her way to visit the men she'd promised to sit with.

Once they arrived in town, Crystal decided to leave Dawn in the fenced in field. It wasn't all that large, but it was a fair size for travelers wishing to give their mounts a comfortable rest while they visited the marketplace or met with friends and family. Dawn trotted into the center of the field, where a few bales of hay had been untied and left for travelers' horses to replenish themselves.

She loved the fact the townspeople and country folk cared enough for the animals to pay for this luxury with their taxes, and as she walked toward the market place, she felt content knowing her horse was safe.

Crystal meandered through town with her fistful of flowers. They were no worse for wear after their trip in one of Dawn's saddlebags. She wanted to visit the pottery shop, in hopes of finding a deal on some small, decorative vases. There were only six men, and she figured she'd let the shop owner know of her intent before purchasing his goods. She just wanted something for the flowers to be able to sit in, to give them some beauty to look at between her visits.

The table out front of the pottery shop filled with wares

available for purchase had several beautiful options for her flowered gifts. There were a set of eight small vases, each done in a different color but all with the same designs of swirls and falling petals. There were more than she required, but their sizes would be perfect for what she had in mind.

She glanced up, searching for the vendor and finding him on the other side of the long table helping an elderly woman pick out some dinnerware. While she waited, she browsed the other items, but none of them spoke to her in the way the set of smaller vases had. She knew she wanted them, and while she intended to hunt for the deal, she figured she'd be happy enough to pay the older man who ran the shop whatever amount he asked.

"Good day to you, miss! How can I help you today?" he asked her, his weathered skin bunching up around his eyes as his smile broke across his face. His brown eyes sparkled with joy as he dropped his gaze to the item before her; the set of small vases.

"I wanted to go visit the soldiers who hadn't been claimed at the sick house. I spent some time with them yesterday afternoon when I was searching for my love who hadn't yet returned to me from the wars, but I didn't want to show up empty handed today." She lifted her fisted palm of flowers. "I picked these from my own garden before I left home, but I didn't have anything to place them in so that they could perhaps brighten their rooms and spirits some. They were wounded something awful fighting for our easy way of life, it just broke my heart to see them dying alone like they are."

"I probably have something that would work quite well for your needs," the vendor replied. He pulled a small crate from beneath the table. "You can use this to carry whatever you choose over to the sick house. Did you manage to find him; your love, I mean?"

A pain throbbed in her chest where her heart lay, she inhaled a breath at the shock. She hadn't yet come to terms with the fact her love would never return to her, and the reminder had hit her when she hadn't expected. Glancing down at the vases she knew she wanted, she answered, "No. I'm afraid my soldier won't be returning to me."

A sigh escaped the man on the other side of the table as he scratched his nearly balding head. Crystal tried to ignore the pity shining in his eyes and, instead of acknowledging her sorrow, she pointed at the eight vases before her.

"These would be perfect. They are small enough not to require too many flowers, but beautiful enough to brighten the room even should the flowers be missing between my replacing them. Would you be willing to strike a deal, seeing as they're for the unclaimed soldiers who fought for our freedom?"

She felt bold asking him that as she pinned him with a hard stare, unblinking while he contemplated her words. She watched him as he stared across his wares at her, his bottom lip twitching as he chewed it. Suddenly, he smiled and chuckled.

"You make a hard bargain," he said, still laughing a deep rich sound. "I'll tell you what. I'll sell you the set for the price of two of these. What do you say?"

She smiled. "It's a deal."

One of the six men had passed during the night. Crystal sent up a silent prayer to aid his soul's trip home. She visited four others before visiting the man she'd started with yesterday.

She'd had a lengthy pleasant chat with a man who'd lost his eye, part of his nose, an ear, and an arm. He'd been standing too closely to a blast of air magic and had lost a good part of his face for his troubles.

Each of the men she'd visited had smiled at the small vase of flowers she brought them, and she'd left all of the drapes covering their windows open a crack. Lying in the dark all day and all night would do nothing to lift their spirits and help them fight for their lives.

Finished chatting small talk with the four men, she made her way to the soldier whose sadness and hopelessness had moved her to promise future visits with the wounded and forgotten men on the second floor of the sick house. She hadn't realized it until now, but she was oddly looking forward to this visit.

She pushed the door open and entered, wrinkling her nose slightly at the stench. She walked across the room with the remaining vase of flowers, she had left the extra vase in the crate outside the door, and placed the vase on his bedside table.

Then she wrenched open the drapes and opened the window to let in some fresh air, causing the man in the bed to stir.

Pulling over a chair from along the wall, Crystal sat down next to his bed. "I told you I'd be back," she said with a smile.

His eyes flicked from her to the vase of flowers to the open window letting in bright sunlight. He groaned as he turned over in the bed, into a more comfortable position to face her and visit. He tapped his throat a few times, his mouth opening and closing like a fish as he glanced to the sink along the wall next to the door.

"Water?" she asked.

When he nodded, she rose to her feet and crossed the room, filling a glass from the small cabinet above the sink with fresh, cold water. She noticed straws in a cup in the cupboard and grabbed one, bending it as she made her way back to his side. She sat and leaned forward, holding the straw to his lips until he finished pulling water into his parched throat. When he finished, he started making growling noises in the back of his throat.

"Y-You c-c-came ba-back," he stuttered, his voice sounding rough and dry and unused.

She grinned at him as she set the cup onto the bedside table next to her. "Of course, I did! I told you I would. Can you tell me your name?"

"L-L-Logan. And y-you are?" he struggled to make his weak voice heard, but she could understand him well enough.

"My name is Crystal Mayberry."

"D-Did Did you find th-the man—"

"—No," Crystal interrupted with a sad shake of her head. "No, I'm afraid I didn't."

Logan's face fell. "I-I-I'm sorry to hear th-that," he replied, heartfelt.

Crystal pointed to the vase she'd brought in, this one a lovely teal and silver color with dark blue cornflowers and crisp white petunias. She waited for Logan's gaze to drift toward her gift before speaking. "I brought you something to brighten your room up some."

The corner of his lips lifted in a small smile, and his eyes filled with joy. A content sigh slipped from his chapped lips, and he looked up at her adoringly.

"Did you have someone waiting for your return who you wish me to fetch for you?" she asked him. She might not be able to find her lover returned from the wars, but there was no reason he couldn't return to his, if he so desired.

His chin dropped to his chest as he sadly shook his head. When he looked back into her eyes, the loss looking back at her overwhelmed her and broke her heart before he even spoke the words.

"I left her preg-pregnant and I am afraid..." He paused to compose himself, the words he spoke making him emotional. "I'm afraid sh-she didn't survive the birth of our son."

Crystal brought her hand to her heart as she gasped. She couldn't imagine hearing that kind of news while battling in the king's army in far away lands. The heartbreak he must have felt! And to still be required to fight for the people's safety from the dark sorcerers. She admired the strength that must have taken, and she looked down at his withered form proudly.

His clear blue gaze latched onto hers, and she couldn't tear her eyes away from him. Burns and scars covered the majority of his face, hiding his identity from those who didn't know him. Though, the real reason he had been given a room on the second floor of the sick house broke her heart. He'd had no one left to claim him.

"I will visit you everyday until you're better. Would that be okay with you?" she asked, reaching forward to grip his hand in hers. There were no burns on his fingers, and so she could cause him no more pain with her gentle touch.

"You don't have to do that," he replied, his voice strengthening the more he spoke. It still sounded gravelly, but to hear him speak made her happy with his progress.

"No, I don't. But I'm terribly lonely without my love. You'd actually be doing me a favor by letting me visit. It will give me something to do. Otherwise, I'm afraid I may become lost within my grief," she answered him honestly.

His eyes flicked to the doorway and then back up to her face. "Can we be heard in here?" he whispered, his fingers gripping hers tightly.

"No. The nurses rarely come up here. They believe you all to be a lost cause. Though, I believe you can live."

Logan smiled at her, his teeth pristine white and straight. He had a gorgeous grin, she noticed. "I've heard tales of women who could raise the dead. While I was in Embrasia, we came upon a sorcerer's tower. It was shortly after I'd received news of Angela and our son. We were sent into the tower to eliminate the threat within, but I'd found some documents detailing some parchments required in the study of necromancy."

The last of his words came out as mostly air, and so Crystal let go of his hand to bring the glass of water near enough to his lips for the straw to slip into his mouth. He pulled long and hard until he'd emptied the glass, and then he pinned her with a hard stare. His brow rose, though there was no eyebrow left from the burns he'd suffered.

"Why are you telling me this?" she asked, setting the glass down again.

"Isn't it obvious? If you help me to live, I want to help you raise your lover."

CHAPTER FIVE

THE SET UP

Two weeks later...

CRYSTAL WALKED INTO THE SICK HOUSE THE same time she had the past several days, shortly before noon with a brown paper bag lunch for Logan. She still spent time visiting the remaining soldiers on the second floor, but as she walked into the main room and nearly passed the receptionist's desk, the head nurse stood and held a hand in the air to halt her forward momentum. Crystal twisted on her heel and walked toward the desk to see what the woman wanted.

"You're the woman who's been visiting the unclaimed soldiers?"

Crystal nodded.

"I'm afraid three more passed away during the night. I just thought you should know; I didn't want you to be caught off guard when you went to visit them. And can I just say: What you are doing is absolutely admirable."

Crystal waved her left hand. "It really isn't," she replied. "Honestly, it's probably the most selfish thing I've ever done."

The head nurse smiled with a shake of her head, her tight red curls swinging in her high ponytail. "I doubt that completely," she said. "You're giving them peace in their final days. Though that one lad, what's his name again?"

"Logan."

"Yes, him. I actually think he may survive his wounds. You've given him something to live for it seems." The nurse smiled, her violet eyes twinkling.

"Can I get a nurse?" a feminine voice called from somewhere down the hall, panic laced within her tone.

"I better go see what that's about. You can see yourself upstairs, right?"

"Of course," Crystal answered, stepping away from the desk and making room for the head nurse to rush past her to check on things in her sick house.

After visiting the soldiers for the past two weeks, she knew exactly where she needed to go. She climbed the stairs to the second floor and stopped at the beginning of the hallway. If what the nurse had said was true, which she doubted the nurse would lie about such things, the rest of her wounded soldiers had left this world for the next, since another had lost his fight only a few days prior. She took a moment to mourn their losses and sent a silent prayer to the gods above, it would be up to them to watch over her soldiers now.

Shaking her grief from her thoughts, she put a smile on her face before cracking Logan's door open. The smell had eased over the days, as his wounds healed slowly. The burns had gone down in redness, and now his skin had a more pinkish hue, almost as if a blush had covered his entire face. His voice barely sounded scratchy and hoarse, his mood had lifted, and he had begun eating solid foods days ago. Peeking into the room, she could see Logan where he lay in his sick bed as he lifted his fingers in a tiny wave.

She shoved the door the rest of the way open and entered the room with a genuine smile stretched across her face. Crystal placed the brown paper bag on the bedside table before shrugging out of her brown leather jacket and hanging it over the chair as she brought it closer to Logan's bedside.

"Did you bring any more?" Logan asked, the anticipation evident as he leaned forward.

Laughing, Crystal drew the small glass bottle from the pocket of her maroon, floor-length skirts and twisted it back and forth in the air to show him she had. She sat in the chair and scooted closer to his side as she twisted the cork free from the bottle and dumped some of the cold, lilac hued cream into the palm of her hand. Setting the bottle on the table next to her, she waited for him to lean closer.

"This stuff is gold! Where did you find it?" Logan's eyes lit with his excitement as he moved closer to the edge of his sick bed easily.

She rubbed the cool cream into the wounds on his face, massaging it gently into the skin and letting her fingers trail the elixir down his neck to cover the remaining burns of his neck, shoulder, and back. He lay with his eyes closed and a small smile lifting his lips as he waited for her to finish.

The cream itself had no smell, but it felt smooth as silk on her fingers, and once it had been rubbed into his skin until no evidence of it remained, it made his skin appear smoother, less red and rigid from the sorcerer's burns he'd suffered. With any luck, the cream would do what she was told it would and heal his wounds as if nothing had ever happened.

Standing, Crystal walked to the sink in the corner of the room and washed her palms clean of the cream. She dried her dripping hands in the folds of her skirts as she made her way back to his side.

"I went to the old hag out by the swamp," Crystal replied finally.

Logan's eyes went wide. "You went out there alone? You shouldn't have!"

She waved a hand at him. "Nonsense. Honestly, I bet the townsfolk say just as awful things about me living on my own out in the hills."

She crossed her legs and adjusted her skirts to fall properly around her lifted leg. She brought her fingertips to trail across the skin of his cheek. Last week, there had been welts lifted and wrinkling the skin that had been raw, red, and charred black in places. This week, the welts had subsided some and the hue had gone down to that of an angry sunburn.

He lifted a brow in question.

She sighed, letting her fingers fall back to her lap. "You think I shouldn't have gone to the old hag because there are rumors that she's an old witch doctor? If she were dangerous, don't you think the king would have had his army dispose of her during the dark wars? Honestly, she's just misunderstood because she prefers to be left alone by the swamp. Not unlike me and my lonely rolling hills I surround myself with."

Logan reached out, gripping her hands into his larger hold and bringing them to his lips. He kissed them gently, his gaze never leaving hers. "I could never think such fearful thoughts about you. I'm sure you are right about the old hag. How did you know to go to her?" he asked, holding her fingers above his heart while he listened intently to what she had to say.

"I knew I had to do something. The nurses here have only been keeping you comfortable, they haven't been doing anything to actually aid your healing. I'd heard rumors of the old hag being a witch doctor and figured it was as good a place as any to start looking for ways to heal you," Crystal explained. She left out the part where she had vague memories of her mother talking fondly of the swamp hag, which filled Crystal with an instinct to just trust the woman.

Just then, a knock sounded at the open door, and when

Crystal turned to see who'd interrupted their chat, she noticed the head nurse from earlier standing in the doorway with a clipboard gripped in one hand and a pen in the other. Crystal smiled at the nurse while she discreetly slipped the elixir back into the pocket of her skirt. She didn't know what the nurses would think of it, and seeing how the king had just finished warring against sorcerers, she didn't want to chance it.

Logan reached for the brown paper bag and opened it, peering inside as the nurse came into the room. "Sir, is it okay with you if I discuss your medical information in front of your visitor?" the nurse asked as she stepped next to the bed.

Logan nodded as he pulled an apple from the bag and bit into it, crumpling the top of the bag closed and placing it back onto his bedside table as he fixed the nurse with a stare. Crystal twisted in her seat until she half-faced the nurse and still half-faced where Logan lay next to her.

"You've healed better than anyone here had expected. It must either be the power of miracle, or the power of having something to live for," the nurse paused to glance at Crystal before continuing, "Whatever the reason, the staff at this sick house has decided you should be well enough to leave within the next few days. It's time you begin to make arrangements for where you will be heading next."

Logan looked to Crystal, a half-grin plastered to his face as he grabbed her hand and gave it a squeeze. He glanced back to the nurse before speaking. "I'm not sure where I'll be headed. I have some things to figure out it seems."

"Nonsense. If you would like, you're more than welcome to move in with me until you're back on your feet one hundred percent," Crystal replied.

Not only did they have a deal, but she had begun thinking of Logan as a friend over the past weeks since she'd been visiting. At first, she'd wanted what was best for him because it seemed the quickest way to reach what was best for her. Now, though, she truly cared for the man's well-being. She'd started something that day just over two weeks ago, something that had bloomed with her gift of flowers into the beginning of a wonderful friendship.

He nodded happily.

"That's wonderful news!" the nurse exclaimed. She jotted notes down on the clipboard as she spoke. "Perfect! I'll just need a few details from you on your way out this afternoon then, miss." She gave them both a slight smile, pleased that her patient would continue to be looked after once he was released, and then left them alone again.

Logan took another bite of the apple, juices dripping down his chin. Crystal leaned forward to wipe it away with her thumb and gasped when Logan quickly grabbed her wrist and plopped her thumb into his mouth, sucking the juices from her delicate skin. She pulled her hand from his grip and scolded him playfully.

"Now, now! Is that anyway to treat your new roommate?" she questioned, smiling.

His light blue eyes twinkled with mischief as he bit into the apple once more. As he chewed, he replied with a wink, "I guess only time will tell."

"Watch your step. Careful. I've got you," Crystal said as she guided Logan into her house. He had his arm looped around her neck, and hers wrapped around his waist as she helped him up the steps of her front porch.

Both of her horses still stood out front of her house, attached to the carriage she'd hooked them to in order to retrieve their new guest. She'd have to get Logan settled before returning to release them from where they'd been left.

As they came to her front door, she propped Logan up against the wall while she pulled her keys from her pocket and unlocked the door, swinging it open to give them entrance. Logan stood and waltzed through the door as if he hadn't just spent the last four and a half weeks confined to a sick bed. Crystal's mouth dropped as she stood frozen on the threshold.

"Well, aren't you going to come in?" he asked when he noticed her still standing at the door, his gaze sweeping across her entrance and adjoining living room. "Wow, this is a nice place!"

She stormed into the room until she stood in front of him, jabbed her finger into his chest, and scolded, "You made me do all that work to get you into the carriage and back out of it, and you can walk just fine? What the hell?"

He brushed away the spot she'd poked with mock disgruntlement, a crease cutting a path between his brow, which now had fresh eyebrows growing back in, as he looked up into her furious gaze. "Of course, I did! You were so cute when you were determined to help me walk, I didn't want to let you down by not needing your help." He grinned, twirling on his heel and walking further into the house. "So, how about a tour?"

Sighing, she pushed past him, giving him a slight glare as she did so. She wasn't angry, in fact, she was almost amused at his tactics. Though, she didn't plan to let him in on that anytime soon.

"Through this hallway, we have the kitchen. Through here, next to the stairway, is the main floor bathroom. Follow me," she said, heading for the stairs. She gave him a look. "I'm assuming stairs won't be a problem for you, either."

She led the way upstairs, hearing him chuckle at her assumption. The upstairs was just as cozy as the main floor, with only a bedroom, a spare bedroom, and a larger bathroom. A closet sat next to the bathroom door, which she filled to the brim with her linens and seasonal things. She showed him to the guest room, which she told him he could use for as long as he needed, and then she showed him the bathroom and from where to collect fresh linens.

"What's that room then?" he asked, and she could swear there was a twinkle in his eye. He moved as if he were heading toward the closed door.

She brought a hand up and placed it on his chest, stopping him from getting any closer. "Nice try, Casanova. Come on, let's go back downstairs. I'll brew us some coffee and we can figure out where to go from here."

He sighed dramatically. "I guess the answer to that won't be what's behind door number three?" he asked, his eyes flicking to her closed bedroom door again.

"Not a chance," she said, leading the way back downstairs.

Once they both made it back down to the main floor, she motioned for Logan to have a seat in one of the high-backed white sofa chairs she had angled toward the fireplace while she knelt before the hearth and set a single log burning low. She didn't need to keep the house warm, the weather hadn't yet turned cold enough outside to warrant that, but there was something about sitting in front of a flickering flame that just made the room cozier to her.

"Make yourself at home," she said as she straightened from the hearth, dusting her fingers on her skirt as she crossed the room. She gesticulated toward the shelves of books she'd stopped next to. "If you want to read while you wait, I won't be but a moment."

He raised a brow at her as he leaned forward, curious. "Where are you going?"

"To stable the horses."

"Hmph," Logan moaned as he leaned back in the chair, the dancing flames lighting his gaze as he watched the hearth.

Crystal slipped outside and unhitched the horses from the

carriage once she'd parked the small vehicle next to her home. Once she'd had both horses back into their stalls with fresh oats and water, she hurried back inside, being sure to grab something of Logan's from the carriage before making her way to the front of her house. She wasn't sure what their plan would be now that Logan had been released from the hospital, but she intended to figure that out before they went to their separate beds tonight. Knowing would put her mind at ease.

When she came through the front door, the scent of coffee filled her cozy home. Logan came out of the kitchen holding two large ceramic mugs with steam climbing in a dancing pattern through the air. He held one out to her with a wink.

She pulled his now-empty vase from where she'd been holding it behind her back and offered a trade as she came up to him and took the drink he held out to her. His fingers brushed against hers as he pulled the empty ceramic vase from her hold, sending a shiver singing through her blood at the contact.

She pulled her hand away and turned toward the living room, sitting in one of the chairs facing the stone fireplace. A small rounded end table sat nestled between the two chairs in which they sat, and Crystal placed her steaming mug down between them as she twisted in her chair to face Logan.

He blew across the top of his coffee before sipping noisily from his cup, and then he followed suit and placed the cup between them. She watched him, waiting for him to start, and when he didn't, she probed.

"So? What's the plan then?"

"Hmmm? Oh, yes. The Plan." He scratched at the whiskers beginning to grow on his chin. "To raise your dead lover, you mean?"

She rolled her eyes. "Yes! What other plan is there?"

Logan's attentions had been nice after so long of feeling nothing but loneliness as she awaited the return of her Brent, but he wasn't Brent. She missed the way Brent's hair always tickled her nose when she kissed him, how it felt silky smooth in her fingers as she brushed his messy locks away from his angular face. When Logan had said he'd help her bring her lover back, she became determined to do just that.

Logan bent forward suddenly, tugging at the laces of his army boots. She wondered what in the five kingdoms he was doing as she watched him pull the beige boot from his foot. When his hand shot into the toe of the boot, she wrinkled her nose at him as a look of disgust crossed her face.

"What *are* you doing?" she wondered aloud, making Logan pause what he was doing to peer up at her.

When he saw the disgruntled look marring her features, he chuckled and then continued digging into the toe of his worn boot.

"Ah, there it is!" he exclaimed as his fingers wrapped around something deep within the footwear. He pulled his arm free and revealed the—extremely dirty—folded up sheets of paper.

Crystal pinched her nose at the smell permeating the air,

waving a hand in front of her face as if to fan away the odor.

"Yup, those are ripe!" Logan chuckled, offering the pages to Crystal, who shook her head vehemently. "I guess they are a bit nasty, huh?"

Cupping her hands around her nose and mouth, Crystal spoke. "How long have those been in there for? And what *are* they?" Her voice sounded nasally and muffled.

"These are the pages from the tower I managed to hide away unseen. I told you, it was during a time I'd been mourning the loss of my own love. When I read a bit of the documents and they mentioned 'Raising the Dead,' I grabbed them. Back at the base, I stuffed them where I knew no one would look. They've been in the bottom of my boot for the last seven months."

"Do you want us to raise your love as well?"

Logan shook his head sadly while he tried to flatten the sheets out in a manner that they'd be able to read. He glanced up, his clear blue eyes searching hers before he replied, "No. I lost a son as well. She's needed in the next world to keep our boy safe."

"Then why did you hold on to those," she said, pointing at the documents he was still straightening on his lap, "for all this time?"

He expelled a large breath of air as he thought of a response, his fingers stilling on the parchment. "I suppose I don't really know anymore."

"Why do you want to help me?"

He turned to face her then, the pages in order now, and smiled that dazzling smile of his. His soft, pink lips opened as he dragged the tip of his tongue across them to wet them. She tried not to let his movements turn her on; she was discussing raising her dead lover, not exactly an appropriate time to be falling for another man's charms.

"That's simple, love. You helped me survive wounds that would have ended my life from the sheer hopelessness of my situation. So, in other words, I owe you my life."

Logan reached for his mug between them, and as he did, she placed a hand over his. He glanced up into her emerald green eyes, his one brow raised in question.

"Thank you, Logan, for giving me the hope I needed to survive. I think you saved my life just as much as you feel that I have saved yours." She pulled away then, reaching for her own cup of coffee and sipping the now-warm contents.

Logan cleared his throat, as if the emotion in the room had become too heavy for him.

She smiled, knowing they had saved each other that day not so long ago, when she'd gotten the news that had shattered her heart. With each other's help, perhaps they'd be able to piece their broken hearts back together.

"So, your plan is for us to become Necromancers?" Crystal asked, her lips puckered as she waited for his response.

He took a long pull from his own mug before replying, "Precisely, my dear."

CHAPTER SIX

THE SEARCH FOR KNOWLEDGE

CRYSTAL STOOD IN THE MIDDLE OF A ROOM, OR what she figured must be a room, she couldn't really tell since her eyes had been covered with a scarf. She and Logan had ridden into town on her horses, penned them, and had walked through the markets until coming to a side street somewhat out of the way of the wandering people out on this fine, warm day. Once they'd moved from where the crowds shopped, he'd pulled a teal scarf from the pocket of his jacket and stole her sight. Now, he was off doing who knew what within wherever he had led her. Switches flicked around the room, fabric swayed from behind her, and his footsteps slowly approached.

Placing his hands on her shoulders, he turned her around until she faced him. She felt his arms wrap around her, the heat from his body warming hers as they stood too close for Crystal's comfort, his intoxicating scent filling her senses while his fingers twisted at the fabric tied behind her head as he released her blindfold.

As the scarf fell from her face, she reached to catch it, her fingers grazing his chest, which felt solid beneath the thin, lime-green fabric of his button-up shirt. She sucked her lip into her mouth as she stepped back, taking a moment to calm her breathing while hoping her skin hadn't betrayed the chemistry flaring to life between them.

"So? What do you think?" he asked, his eyes sweeping across the room in which they stood, a goofy smile plastered to his face.

The room seemed to be a fair size, with the look and feel of a homey, wooden cottage. No furniture filled the space, it was as if its owners had vacated the place ages ago, as a layer of dust covered the redwood hardwood floors, windowsills, and the set of stairs that climbed to a second-floor loft in a spiral manner. A closed door sat along the farthest wall, and a counter cut a window into the wall a few feet from the door. Through the window, a small kitchen stretched along the back of the house, with a large arched doorway along the wall of the hallway, which must be what sat behind the closed door she'd noticed.

"This is the main room, I figured we could line the walls with shelves, maybe put in a long counter along that front wall there, and we could fill the rest of this space with bookcases as well. The fact that that kitchen has a window into this room has me thinking of a small coffee shop type area, we could even offer pastries if we wanted. There's a bathroom down that hallway too, every little shop needs one of those. And up there," he said as he pointed to the loft, his eyes filled with his excitement as his words rushed from him, "we can have a section of rare books, the books we'll need to finish our task."

"What are you talking about?"

She stopped looking at the home he'd brought her to and cocked a brow at him. She had no idea where any of this had even come from. They'd come to town to grab provisions for another few days, not to... well, whatever this was. She wasn't buying a house with Logan! She had her own perfectly acceptable home, away from all the townsfolk who hadn't made her childhood enjoyable at all. Sometimes, when she'd been in the silence too long, she could still hear their jeers about being the daughter of the palace's help.

He grinned, admiring the room in which they stood. "This is ours!" he stated proudly.

"What?" Her jaw dropped. "Why would you do this? I love my house. I like being outside the town walls. I enjoy my privacy. I don't want this!" she exclaimed.

How much did a place in town even cost? How could he afford something like this? He'd been on sick leave and dispelled from the king's army when he'd been wounded.

Logan came forward, placing his hands on her shoulders and squeezing them as he dipped his head to peer into her emerald green eyes. Concern etched a crease between his brows as he made soothing noises before speaking, "Shhh. Calm down; it's not what you're thinking. It's part of our plan. I haven't lost sight of our end goal, Crystal. Promise."

She breathed deeply before lifting her gaze to meet his. "What part of the plan is this then?"

"We need to get our hands on some texts that would otherwise raise suspicions. What better way to gather and collect said texts than by opening a bookshop?" He watched her process his words.

A slow smile stretched her thin lips and she smacked him playfully in the arm. He raised his brows at her gentle tap. "For the record, maybe you should lead with the whole, 'Want to go into business together,' thing instead of leading a woman into an empty home blindfolded and then telling her it now belongs to you both."

Loud laughter rang around the room as Logan held his gut and bent forward. When he stood, he wiped tears from his eyes. The sounds he filled the air with had her keeling over, her own fit of giggles spilling out from her. For a minute there, he'd had her worried. She wasn't ready to let Brent go, not yet. After several moments, they finally regained their composure, a few last chuckles escaping them as they straightened.

She pushed past him saying, "I'm glad I amuse you so," and then made her way to the bottom of the spiral, metal staircase in the back corner of the room.

She didn't look behind her as she climbed upward, her fingers trailing along the cold, somewhat rusted, metal railing. The second floor came out over half of the main floor, with a railing, which matched the staircase, along the drop to the main room. She hated to admit it, but Logan's vision for the place wasn't half bad. The loft would be perfect for a restricted section of rare books and texts, there was even enough room up here for a large table, which would come in handy when it came time to study the texts for what they required.

Making her way toward the railing along the edge of the loft, she peered down to search for Logan, but he no longer stood where she'd left him. A gasp escaped her, and a smile curved her lips as she felt his arms snake around her waist to hold onto the railing, effectively caging her between his grasp. He rested his chin on her shoulder, the five o'clock shadow he seemed to enjoy maintaining tickling her cheek as he breathed in the floral scent of her hair.

"So?" he asked simply.

She turned around in his hold, smiling up at him. She'd always loved books, and she had no doubt that she could turn this into a quaint little shop, but could she truly accept this gift he offered? Worry creased her brow, making Logan lift his hand to cup her face, his thumb smoothing the wrinkle gently.

"What's wrong? If you don't like it, there are a few other buildings we could look at. I'm sure the king wouldn't mind if we changed our mind. We can do whatever you want, just tell me what you're thinking so I can help," he said, his words soft and full of concern.

"It's not that. I love it! I'm just not sure I can accept this from you. How much did this place even cost?"

"I don't want you to worry about a thing, Crystal. I was discharged from the king's army because I'd fallen wounded in battle, a war he sent his soldiers to fight. I'm doing well financially, actually. I want to do this for you. Besides, after we accomplish our goal, I'm going to need a place to live. So, if you're happy with this place, then it's ours," Logan explained, his clear blue eyes watching her intently.

She chewed her lip a moment while she thought it over, her chin dipping to her chest, unable to hold his caring gaze. It was clear he had feelings for her, feelings she continued to fight on her end.

He'd healed perfectly, with no trace of the burns he'd suffered during the wars, but it wasn't just his appearance she was attracted to, it was his soul. Maybe it was because he thought she'd saved his life, and maybe she had, but he seemed intent on doing whatever it took to make her happy. A girl could get used to a feeling like that.

Finally, she lifted her head to meet his stare. "Then I accept. This place will be perfect," she replied, reaching up on her tiptoes to place a chaste kiss to his cheek. She pulled away before he had a chance to hold onto her for more.

As she made it to the top of the stairs, she turned to face him once more. "I hope you know a thing or two about opening up this kind of a shop though, because I haven't the faintest idea," she said with a shrug, then she skipped down the staircase, leaving Logan to admire her retreating form.

It took them four weeks to figure all the details out, during which Logan spruced the place up to ready it for its Grand Opening. Crystal had passed out sheets advertising their Grand Opening, boasting books, coffee, and pastry treats to anyone interested in helping them celebrate the start of their journey. Logan had re-stained all the wooden surfaces a cherry-wooden hue, he'd fastened shelves along all the walls and created aisles throughout the space as well, he'd replaced all the lighting with modern chrome fixtures to ensure reading ease, and he built a wonderful counter and purchased an old fashioned cash register. As Crystal twirled around the room an hour before their opening, she couldn't believe how well everything had turned out for them.

"You know what this place is missing?" she asked Logan, her lips pinched into a thin line as she surveyed their surroundings.

"I hope it's nothing major; we'll be entertaining people shortly..."

A slow, teasing smile curved her glossy pink lips. "Nothing," she said matter of factly, hugging Logan.

"Did you see the shipment of books that just came in this morning?" he asked her, pulling away with his arms still wrapped around her waist while he gazed down into her emerald green eyes. When she shook her head, he continued, "They look like ancient texts that may turn to dust with our touch, but if we're careful, they could have some useful information."

They had already begun collecting texts and parchment rolls with the details of raising people from the dead. They hadn't found any how-tos on the topic yet, but she knew it was only a matter of time. Most of what they'd found so far just mentioned the possibility of necromancy, and then, of course, were the stacks of books they'd purchased on the topic that were purely fiction. Every time another book they'd pinned their hopes onto made its way to the shop only to be fictional was a let down, but with their Grand Opening today, they'd soon have no issues with moving those titles from their shelves.

"Are you talking about the ones with the metal clasps and bound in old, chipping leather?"

"Those are the ones," he replied.

"I did see them on the counter before you squirreled them away upstairs. Nice job on the 'Employees Only' gate you welded for the bottom of the staircase by the way," she praised. They didn't need people poking their noses into their intentions. "We'll have to check them out once we close up shop."

A timer went off in the kitchen and she pulled free of Logan's hold. She had a few things left to pop into the oven before their patrons arrived, setting the stage of their quaint little shop for the future. They needed to make a good impression; the texts for which they searched were quite pricey, the funds they earned from selling books and café goods would funnel back into their search. She refused to let Logan pay for everything with the coin the king had paid him for his injuries and dismissal from his army.

"I have a few things left to finish up in the kitchen. Why don't you make sure everything out here is in order?" she asked, back-pedaling her way toward the hallway leading to the kitchen. When he nodded, she turned and began working on the final set-up.

They'd purchased beautiful baskets from the weaver, which she intended to have sitting on the counter between the kitchen and the main shop, filled with her baked goods. She already had a few set up with different flavors of muffins; chocolate chip, blueberry, banana, Dargonia berry. The timer she'd heard before meant her pies were ready, and she pulled them free of the heat to cool while she threw in the trays of cookies she'd prepared. While waiting for the pies to cool, she began brewing a pot of coffee in each of her three machines, readying more filters with grounds to save time should she need to brew more once they began pouring into the glass carafes.

A small table sat next to the window, on which she had stacked little parchment paper bags, napkins, and a small cash register for café purchases. A tiny chalkboard menu hung next to the window on the wall of the main shop, listing the goods she'd prepared along with the prices, which were low enough to be attractive but high enough to cover her costs and garner her a small income.

On busy days, the place would require two workers, which would be perfect for the two of them, but on slower days, one of them would be able to manage the place on their own just fine. They expected today to be quite busy with the amount of hype she'd caused out in the markets over the past week. After the initial rush, she expected business to slow down quite a piece; not everyone would be interested in purchasing books everyday, though the café may bring in its own customers. Only time would tell.

Once they opened their doors, the customers provided a steady distraction from their hunt. After a few hours, Crystal's body ached in places she didn't realize existed, and she began looking forward to a warm bubble bath later to ease her sore muscles. Some of her scented lavender candles, the bath salts that fizzed the water, and her fluffiest towel rolled for her neck... She still had several hours left before she intended to head back home, but damn it all to hell if she didn't want to head there now.

With time passing as fast as it was, the constant state of busy helping to speed things up, it wasn't long before Logan slipped into the kitchen and came up behind her, his arms wrapping around her waist as she continued mixing the batter for tomorrow's treats. She twisted her head to peer up at him, and he wiped flour off her cheek with his thumb.

"We did it," he said, his eyes sparkling.

"Are we done?" she asked.

Her feet ached something awful, and she really just wanted to pop her batters into the fridge and pick up where she left off in the morning.

"We are. We did great for our first day. I think we make a great team."

She turned in his arms until she faced him, his hold still circling loosely around her hips. He beamed down at her with such pride, and it had been so long since a man had looked at her the way Logan looked at her now. She loved Brent, but he'd left for the wars what felt like ages ago. She'd been on her own for over a year before she'd found Logan. Yes, she still had every intention of raising Brent, but would she be able to keep her heart guarded from Logan?

She could tell he wanted her, even though they planned to learn necromancy in order to bring her lover back from the dead. It just made her heart melt more knowing that though. Still, she put up her walls and stepped out of his hold, making sure there was some space between the two of them.

"We did make a good team," she agreed, "Now, why don't you show me the books you found?"

Hurt flashed across his face before he schooled his features smooth again. She tried to ignore it, but still her heart broke a little knowing she'd caused him that pain. She wasn't ready to let go of Brent though, and she didn't know how to love Brent the way she did when she had started to have feelings for Logan. Until she knew what her heart wanted, she figured it was best to avoid any intimate situations.

Turning, she led the way out of the kitchen. She would come back for her batters later and clean up the kitchen when they'd finished upstairs. She needed to get off her aching feet, and she needed to focus on bringing back Brent. She couldn't do either of those held firmly within Logan's warm and loving embrace, no matter how good it felt or how loud her blood sang its approval in her ears.

Logan had found four new books to start their search with. The parchment he'd pulled from his boot had only listed a few books, but he managed to grab four of the seven. The rest of the page, what they could decipher of it, listed what Crystal believed to be ingredients, though she wasn't really sure.

Logan pulled one of the books from the box and placed it on the table in front of himself; Crystal moved to do the same. The loft had been set up the way they had planned, with shelves lining the walls, a few aisles created with shorter shelves, and a large table with chairs settled somewhere in the middle near the railing overlooking the main floor.

She gripped a thick, leather bound book from the box and pulled it free, sneezing as a cloud of dust danced in the air before her. Whoever they had purchased these from hadn't even bothered to ensure they remained in decent shape.

Crystal trailed her fingers over the cover's golden filigree title: The Art of Necromancing. She'd never seen the word written out like that, and she found it amusing that if you removed the Nec, only romancing remained, which coincidentally was her intention when she began planning to raise her dead lover.

Logan wheeled a chair forward behind where she stood hunched over the large book she'd decided to start with, and she gratefully sat down, smiling up at him as she made herself comfortable. It felt nice getting off her feet finally, and she sighed as her fingers gently worked the brass clasp free so she could open the book. Her nose wrinkled as even more dust rose when the cover fell open, and Logan walked to the back wall of the loft to slide open a window, allowing in fresh autumn air.

"Thank you," she said, "There's so much dust on these books! Where did you get them from anyway?"

He made his way back across the room, pulling a chair out from across the table from her and plopping down with a sigh. It seemed she wasn't the only one with aching feet, she mused. His long fingers worked the clasp while he looked at her with a grimace. "Remember that travelling merchant who set up shop in the market a week ago?"

She nodded, remembering buying all sorts of things from his stall that would aid their own starting business, like those stackable coffee mugs she'd decided to serve coffee in and the trays she'd chosen to display her pies.

"Well, I informed him that I was interested in writing fictional novels based on what I'd seen during the wars, and I told him if he found any dark magical texts to send them our way. I couldn't be too specific because I didn't want to raise the wrong attention, and I had to shelve two of the books he sent over there..." He pointed behind his shoulder, where she noticed two large books, similar to the ones he'd brought to the table, on a shelf by the staircase.

"That was good thinking!" she praised, smiling. "So, what are those two books about then?"

Logan gave her a deadpan look. "You don't want to know."

"Well, I didn't want to until you made it sound all mysterious!"

"Okay, well, don't say I didn't warn you," he replied, with a small shake of his head. "One of them is titled Torture Methods—A Complete Collection, and the other is Fully Utilizing Your Conquests, which had me puzzled enough to open it. I shouldn't have opened it…"

"Why not? What's it about?" Crystal pressed, more curious now than she had been at the start.

"It was graphic, I'll give it that much. It fully depicted the best way to utilize the skin of your sacrifice… your human sacrifice."

Bile rose in Crystal's throat, and she swallowed, trying to shake the unwanted images from her mind.

"I told you that you didn't want to know…"

She held her hand up, stopping his chuckling statement while she squeezed her eyes shut. She breathed deeply for a moment, and when the nausea passed, she fixed him with a hard look. "Okay. That's enough of that, please. Let's move on."

They fell quiet then, studying the texts before them for several hours. With only the sound of old, stiff pages flipping, Crystal read all she could from the book she'd decided to begin with, learning one key element about necromancy. It seemed it didn't matter which spell they found, a few of the ingredients remained the same between spells. This seemed to be good news. She could begin collecting what they would need before they even found a text containing spells.

The only question now was...

Where was she going to find Death's Kiss flower petals, a skull pure of virtue, the talon of a dragon, and whose blood would they use?

CHAPTER SEVEN

THE HUNT FOR INGREDIENTS

THE SUN HAD LONG SINCE SET BY THE TIME THEY made it back to her cozy home in the hills, and the autumn air held a bit more of a chill, sending shivers down Crystal's back. The two of them worked together to treat their horses well as they guided them back to their stalls, brushed them down, and replenished their food and water, stealing glances at each other when they thought they weren't looking.

By the time they made it back into the house, Crystal thought she could feel exactly where every bone and muscle in her chilled body was located, as she throbbed all over, but the tension in her body wasn't the only tension in the room.

"Want some tea?" Logan asked as he made his way inside, hanging his jacket on the peg by the door and kicking off his boots with a groan.

His shirt stuck to his back and chest, dark with sweat and showing, in vivid detail, the lines of his chiseled stomach and chest. The air in the stables was slightly warmer than the night air outside, and Logan had worked harder than she had by lifting fresh bales of hay into each horse's trough.

"Sure. I'm going to go have a soak though," Crystal said, her fingers working a knot out of her neck as she tilted her head.

The heat of the water and the salts she planned to add would make her feel like a whole new woman, and she could almost smell the lavender relaxing her aches already as she peered up the stairs longingly.

Logan gave a half grin before turning from her and heading toward the kitchen. Before he disappeared around the doorway, he said over his shoulder, "I'll get the tea ready then."

As Crystal pulled herself up the stairs by the railing, her back hunching further with every step, she couldn't help but think over the past several weeks. She'd never had a roommate before, her and Brent had been waiting for his return to tie the knot and start their lives together on the proper foot. She couldn't help but enjoy the company of Logan's presence though, or how helpful it was to have a second pair of arms always willing to help her out. It made things easier, or more enjoyable. And, she had to admit, he wasn't hard on the eyes either, which made her heart feel conflicted.

Twisting the taps to her tub, she felt the stream until the temperature was hot enough to burn the first layer of skin clean and leave her pink in hue. As the steam began to billow, she poured various oils and moisturizers into the water, watching as they foamed and frothed into light, airy bubbles. She grabbed the jar of lavender salts from the shelf in the corner and placed it on the edge of the tub, and then she set to work lighting candles all around the room before she flicked the switch and turned off the lights.

When she turned to face the room, a dreamy sigh slipped through her parted lips at the sanctuary she'd created, the floral scents already heavy in the air.

Disrobing took longer than it should have, but with the aches and pains in every joint, she moaned with the movement required to slip free of her ruby red dress and ivory stockings. Leaving her clothes in a heap by the door, she made her way to the tub and dipped a toe into the water.

She hissed as the heat kissed her skin, and as she lowered her foot into the water, she groaned in pleasure as the warmth began working out her aches and pains. She'd been looking forward to this all day.

She leaned her head back onto her rolled, fluffy white towel, her hair falling from her ponytail in rich-brown ringlets, the moisture in the air causing her usually straight hair to curl.

Grabbing for the jar she'd left on the edge of the tub, she twisted off the cap and poured some salts into the water. They immediately began fizzing, the bubbles dancing over her body as they filled the room with the relaxing scent of lavender as it mixed with her floral scented bubble mixture.

She let her eyes drift closed as she let the water work its magic. She intended to soak all the heat into her bones and not climb out of the tub until her digits pruned.

When she felt a breeze on her sweaty brow, her eyes popped open to find Logan sneaking into the room. He held a teacup up as if the fact he brought her tea was excuse enough to enter her bathing chambers.

She was just about to tell him she'd drink the tea when she finished her bath, but the words wouldn't come as she watched him make his way to her side. He placed the cup along the edge of the tub and began rolling his lime-green sleeves up to his elbow, a slow, sexy grin growing with each smooth movement he made.

"What do you think you're doing?" she asked, her voice coming out breathier than she intended and not at all as indignant as she'd hoped to sound.

"Finishing what the water started," he replied.

With both sleeves folded up to the elbow, he walked around the tub until he stood over her head. He knelt behind her and lifted a brow, as if to ask for permission.

She didn't know if she'd come to regret this or not, but she sucked her lip in between her teeth and nodded once.

Without further hesitation, he sank his hands into the steamy water and gripped her shoulders in his large grasp. Like an expert, he began massaging the kinks out of her muscles as her head rolled to the side and she moaned in delight.

Bubbles covered the surface of the water and must have teased him with what he knew was beneath the water; she could see his desire behind his light blue eyes as the shade darkened with need. His massaging fingers began edging lower, working out knots in her shoulder blades and back. They slipped to her sides, the tips of his fingers brushing the skin of her breasts, making her breath quicken.

She knew she should stop him, that this wasn't right. If she intended to bring back Brent, then she shouldn't be doing this. She should save herself for Brent's return. She shouldn't give in to her desires. She should grab Logan's hands and tell him that would be enough, put her walls back into place and protect her heart, and his, from when this came to an end, which it would no doubt do once she raised Brent back to her side.

But she'd been alone so long, and it felt good to be wanted again. If she let Logan continue, would it make her unfaithful if her lover was currently dead? Would it?

A thumb brushed one of her nipples and she moaned at the pleasure racing through her blood. Logan brought his lips to her neck, kissing his way up to her earlobe slowly. His teeth pinched her ear and she held her breath, releasing it as he loosed his tongue on her flesh.

His hands continued to roam her body, teasing her more than anything else. She shifted her hips, trying to release some of the tension building between her thighs as she turned to capture Logan's mouth with her own, needing to taste him.

As their lips met and her mouth parted open to give him access, every nerve in her body awakened as his tongue met hers in a kiss that had been building for weeks. She lifted an arm to hold him there, her wet fingers threading through his dark, messy hair.

His fingers began dancing lower, closer to her throbbing core, and her breath hitched with anticipation. As his fingers roamed further, she ached for his touch.

He pulled his mouth from hers, passion heavy in his gaze as he looked down at her adoringly. "Are you okay with this?" he asked in a whisper, as if afraid anything louder may shatter the mood.

Was she okay with this? She'd only ever been with one man before, and she'd promised him she'd wait for his return. How were either of them to predict he wouldn't make it home to her? They'd never discussed that possibility; they'd thought themselves invincible, she supposed. Look where that had gotten them.

She looked into Logan's eyes, seeing the care he held for her burning within them, and as the candles flickered around the room, casting them in a magical glow, and the scents relaxed more than just her muscles, she nodded.

Yes, she wanted to do this. She wanted him; she couldn't deny it. Not in this moment, not as his fingers inched closer and closer to where she most wanted to be massaged.

He grinned down at her before letting his fingers drive her to release.

They had to leave their horses at the edge of the swamp and go the rest of the way on foot. Having made this journey a few weeks ago, Crystal came better prepared this time. She'd barely made it through the swamp in a single day last time, and she figured this time they'd bring provisions and a tent to set up camp. Having Logan along with her helped even the load they both carried, though he had insisted on giving her as light a pack as possible.

It had been a few days since they'd let go of their inhibitions and brought each other to release. The next day, everything had gone back to normal, as if nothing had happened between them at all.

Crystal didn't know if Logan had come to regret his decision, or if she had disappointed him, but the unknowing pushed her further into their task at hand, making her even more determined than before to figure out this necromancy thing.

They'd been walking for nearly an hour in silence, nothing but the sound of the hard ground crunching beneath their boots. As they passed farther and farther into the swamp, the air became thicker and thicker, the heat rising and the humidity becoming strenuous.

It was quite a change from the cool autumn weather to which she'd started to become accustomed. The sweat didn't just dot her forehead, it poured from her hairline in rivulets, and it pooled down her spine, sticking her lilac t-shirt to her back and making the pack on her shoulder seem heavier. She'd already hung her jacket through the strap of her sack, not needing it as the humidity of the swamp became stifling as they continued forward.

The heat effected Logan just as badly, but he'd taken his shirt off and stuffed part of it in the back pocket of his jeans, letting it sway behind him with every step, and his jacket had been stuffed into his pack long before Crystal had removed hers.

She tried not to admire the way the sweat coating his skin highlighted his muscles, and she blamed the dryness in her throat on thirst of water rather than thirst of something else entirely. At least she trailed behind him, where he couldn't see how he affected her, and where she couldn't see the defined edges of his chest and abs. Too bad the weight of the pack on his shoulder had his muscles bulging. She licked her lips as she continued walking.

The sun beat down on them, and the trees barely provided any shade, with almost half of them snapped before their first branches. The area they traversed looked more like a tree graveyard than anything else, with large broken trunks rotting the hard ground.

With every step they took though, Crystal could feel the ground softening, becoming the moist wet land of the swamp. She gazed up at the sky and estimated another five hours of daylight left.

"We should probably stop somewhere nearby to set up camp," Crystal said, panting for breath as she wiped her brow again. What she wouldn't give for a lake or a river, or a birdbath would even do.

Logan didn't stop walking, but he glanced over his shoulder at her and raised a brow.

"Logan, I'm serious."

"We can make it there before the sun starts setting," Logan replied, pushing forward faster.

"Yeah?" she snapped at him. "And how much fun do you think it will be to camp on land covered in a foot of dirty, stagnant water?"

He stopped, letting his head fall backward and peering up at the sky with a sigh.

She waited for him to turn around, and when he did, she knew something was wrong between them.

"What's with you lately?" she pressed, dropping her pack from her shoulder to the ground and sitting on a trunk that had fallen into a perfect, natural bench.

Logan dropped his pack roughly and glared at her. She'd never seen him angry before, to see it now shocked her, and she held her breath as she watched him.

"What's with me? I was about to ask you the same thing!"

"What?"

He tugged at his hair as he sighed, the messy brown length peeking between his fingers.

"We had a magnificent night. Or, at least, I thought we did. But then when it's morning, it was like nothing ever happened between us. It felt like you were ashamed of what happened. I've been giving you your space and you're still upset. I don't know what you want from me!" he exclaimed, tugging at his hair in frustration.

Laughter burst from her throat before she could stop it, and she slammed her hands over her mouth. But his wide-eyed gaze unleashed her giggles even more, until she hugged her middle and bent forward, laughing until she could barely breathe. Wiping tears from her eyes, she said between her giggling, "We were both afraid of the same thing!"

Her response set him to laughing too, and he walked to her side and sat next to her as their laughter died down.

She leaned her head into the crook of his neck, not caring that the sweat matted her hair to her scalp because his skin had a sheen of wetness to it already. They would both require a lengthy wash at the next opportunity.

"I'm not sure what I want, Logan. I want to raise Brent; I need to save him. I promised him I'd wait for his return, and now I feel like I didn't keep my word, but I feel drawn to you in a way I haven't felt before. Not even with Brent.

"But my loyalty has to be to him first, and I want to see this task complete... if you'll still help me?"

She sounded like a madwoman; she knew that. Her words contradicting themselves, her actions confusing to comprehend, and her heart conflicted and being pulled in two separate directions.

He leaned his head down on hers and wrapped his arm around her shoulders. "I guess I can understand that. I owe you my life, and I made you a promise. I will help you raise Brent, but you need to know that I'm falling for you. I think maybe I started falling for you the moment you yanked open the curtains in my sick room. I won't push you to fall into my arms though. I want whatever you want."

She twisted in his arms and looked up at him, her chestnut hair falling into her face with the movement. "Even if I want to be with Brent?"

He brushed her hair behind her ear before replying, "Even if you want to be with Brent. If that's what makes you happy, I won't get in your way. Promise."

She sighed as she straightened, content with his response.

Logan jumped to his feet, grabbed the large pack he'd carried, and tore into it. He glanced at her from where he crouched over the bag and asked, "Should we start setting up our camp now? Or should I hunt for some small game for our dinner?"

She burst out in laughter again and he smiled. "Set up camp, you idiot. I'll throw together a campfire and get dinner started."

Crystal meandered a short distance away from where Logan grunted to himself as he erected a tent large enough for the two of them to spend the night comfortably, searching for dry wood to use for her campfire. With how many dead trees filled the area, she had an armful of twigs, sticks, and small logs in no time.

She dropped the firewood in a pile a few feet away from where Logan had situated the door of their tent and went hunting for stones to use as a fire ring. Several minutes later, she had a decent firepit set up.

Pulling the fire starter from her pack on the ground, she hunched over and nearly began attempting to spark a fire when Logan came up behind her and pulled the tools from her hands.

She glared up at him. "I'm quite capable of starting a fire, you know!"

"Of course, you are, but I can do this while you get the provisions ready," he replied, amused.

Now that they'd worked out their issues, somewhat, they made a good team as they sidestepped around one another while prepping a meal for the both of them.

They sat on the log facing their camp and ate a meal of dried meats, flamed potatoes, and various berries.

As the sun began its fall from the sky, the heat of the day plummeted as well. It wasn't long after that that they were tucking themselves away from the brisk cold and into the tent which would protect them from the elements. They nestled close to one another under the blankets Logan had carried within his pack.

They whispered into the night, talking about everything from the battles he'd fought while in the army to their plans for after they succeeded in their necromancy task. Logan stayed true to his word; he didn't push her for anything more than conversation as he hugged her close for warmth. Crystal just had to figure out if she admired that about him, or if she grieved the loss of his passionate advances.

She'd never been more confused.

Mid-morning the next day, the old hag's hut came into view in the distance. The humidity of the swamp had reached a level of damn near unbearable, and the soles of Crystal's boots began seeping in water hours ago.

Her exhaustion mounted exponentially as every step she took resulted in her boot becoming stuck in the mud, and she was convinced she'd never had a greater workout than the few trips she'd made out to visit the ol' witch doctor.

If Logan struggled just as much as she did, he didn't show it. His skin had a layer of sweat and grime just as it had held yesterday, and she assumed neither of them smelled sweet, though who could tell with the stench of the surrounding swamp? His muscles rippled with each movement, and they'd agreed to leave their camp in place for their return, a decision Crystal grew happier with as her breath wheezed from her exertion.

The conversation stayed light as they marched forward, the sound of their boots suctioning free of the mud ringing loudly around them. They swatted gnats from the air, though Crystal knew she'd inhaled a small handful of the buggers over the hours they'd hiked. She passed it off as extra protein with a shudder every time.

Her laughter filled the air around them at one point when Logan began sputtering curses and spat like a foul-mouthed sailor when some insect or other flew right to the back of his open mouth, effectively halting whatever he'd been about to say in the process.

"Do we have any idea what we're going to say to the swamp sorcerer when we get there?" Logan finally managed, his fingers still wiping spittle from his chin.

She bit her lip to stifle her laughter, took a deep breath, and then replied, "First, I'd advise against calling her a 'sorcerer' as she may take offense, considering the war just waged against magic wielders. Other than that, I'm just going to be honest with her. I don't think I have to hide my intentions from her; she's out casted herself for her own desire for privacy. She won't care one way or the other what I'm trying to do, my only concern is trying to convince her to help me succeed."

The more she thought about it, the more she realized she needed the witch doctor's help. In fact, she doubted she'd be able to raise the dead without some pointers from someone who could wield magic; the little potions and charms the hag managed had to count for something useful. Though, if she really thought about it, she realized she didn't actually know what skills this woman possessed.

She knew she could concoct potions; it's what kept bringing Crystal back over the years. She didn't think any townsfolk even remembered the old hag still resided deep within the swamp, but Crystal had kept tabs on the old woman all these years because she felt a kinship toward the only other outcast she'd ever known. There was that, but there was also the nagging suspicion that her mother and the hag had once been friends.

"Sounds as good a plan as any," Logan replied simply, wiping sweat from his brow with the back of his hand.

They'd be wise to cut a different path home, one which connected with the Quadesian river that cut through the land around Dargonia. She didn't want to even approach her house in the state they both were in now, let alone enter it. The stench they would carry with them would have her airing out her home for a solid week!

They pushed onward, every step making her breath come harder and faster until, finally, she held up an arm and halted their progress. She needed to catch her breath, but the air hanging around them felt too thick for her aching lungs as she wheezed through her teeth, hunched over as if she were about to vomit.

The hut sat a short distance away now, perhaps only minutes further. Crystal didn't want to arrive without the ability to speak, and if she didn't calm her racing heart, that's exactly how she'd show up on the hag's doorstep.

Logan rubbed her back as she remained bent, her hands clenching the stitches in her side as she focused on slowing her breathing. She cringed at the thought of his fingers feeling the thickness of her sweat coating her t-shirt to her shoulder blades, but she had to admit, the gentle motion soothed her speeding heart, and, a few moments later, she stood straight again, his hand falling from her back as she pulled deep breaths into her strained lungs.

"That's a bit better," she said, her voice coming out level and sure instead of winded and weak. She looked sideways into Logan's blue gaze and asked, "Are you ready for this?"

Logan didn't have time to answer because, at that moment, the front door to the old hag's hut banged open, snapping both of their attention to where she stormed from her home, a broom clutched in her fist as if she were ready to shoo rodents away and a look of fury plastered to her scowling face. She swung her arms, and the broom, in the air as she stomped through the mud, dirty water splashing the bottom of her moth-eaten raggedy skirts, toward them yelling profanity. As she approached, her anger dissipated almost instantly.

"Oh. It's just you," she said as she met them where they stood. "What are you doing back here so soon?" She waved a hand as if to tell them to follow her. "Well come on then, the gnats are awful this time of day."

Crystal and Logan shared a look, shrugged, and followed behind the craggily old woman.

As they stepped into the hut, Crystal watched as Logan took in his surroundings. His eyes seemed to widen at the sheer amount of clutter crowding every surface within the small space of the main room. A worn oak table sat near the middle, its surface littered with small bottles, vials, and at least twenty other odd objects Crystal didn't want to look too closely at; she'd learned her lesson on a previous visit that some of the ingredients the old hag used in her creations were better left unseen.

The shelves lining the walls held an array of items, from chicken bones and skulls to jars of eyeballs and teeth, which Crystal had never found the nerve to ask from where she picked up her collection. She wasn't sure she ever wanted to know.

Another bookcase was nestled into the back corner, cobwebs dangling from every corner of the shelves and a layer of dust so thick, she doubted any of the books had been used in the last five years. She wondered if any of those titles would aid her own task, or if the old hag would let her borrow one if she did find a useful tome to peruse.

The old hag waddled her way toward the back of the shack, where a small, dingy kitchen lay in wait. Her form appeared more hunched even from Crystal's last visit a few weeks ago, and she wondered again how old this woman was. She had been an old hag when Crystal had met her years ago, when she was but a little girl still trailing behind her mother's skirts at the market.

Pots and pans began banging as the witch started brewing a pot of tea for her guests, pulling teacups from her cupboards and blowing them clean. Crystal tried not to shudder as she accepted the empty cup and took a seat at the long table in the main room, waiting for the hag to return with a teapot.

She and Logan shared another look while they sat. Crystal tried to brush her cup cleaner with her fingertips discreetly.

Logan leaned closer to her and whispered into her ear, "I wouldn't worry about the cup so much as I'd worry about what's *in* the tea..." His eyes swept the various shelves surrounding the room, his lip curling as his eyes fell on the disgusting jars of oddities.

She pressed her lips into a tight line to hold in her laughter.

He had a point.

The old hag hurried into the room, a worn-down silver tray held between her hands with a steaming cracked teapot, a dish of sugar, and a small canister of milk. She placed the tray between them with a clatter, lifting a silver spoon from the tray to dump a heap of sugar into her own cup before pouring some tea into everyone's mugs. Crystal added nothing to her cup, choosing to drink the tea as is, and Logan simply added a splash of milk before sipping the steaming liquid.

"Well?" the hag broke the silence. "Spit it out, girl! What brings ya?"

Crystal placed her cup down on the table and dropped her hands to her lap, where she wrung them nervously while deciding how best to begin. How exactly did you tell someone you were considering becoming a necromancer?

"She's wanting to raise her suitor from the dead," Logan spit out, sipping his tea.

Well, that was one way to break the ice, she supposed. Not exactly how she'd have done it, but at least it was out in the open now.

The hag scowled across the table at her, making Crystal squirm uncomfortably. "You're messing with the dark arts now, hmm?"

Crystal bristled at that. "No! Well, not really."

"What do you call raising the dead?" the hag pressed.

"I call it not giving up on love," Crystal replied matter-of-factly.

The hag howled, her hand slamming down on the table with her fits of laughter. When she composed herself, she peered across the table at Crystal with a crooked tooth smile. "I've always liked you, girl. All right, tell me what you need from me."

Crystal released the breath she'd been unknowingly holding. "Well, Logan and I," she said, her hand coming to her mouth as she realized something. "Oh, I'm so sorry! I forgot to introduce you two."

"Hello, Logan. You can call me whatever, but most people just call me the old hag," the old woman said with a laugh.

"Okay then. Hello, old hag?" he replied, unsure.

"Exactly!" the hag shouted, then turned her attention back to Crystal. "Carry on, my child."

Crystal finished her tea and put the empty cup back on the table. "We opened a bookshop to be able to do the research we figured we'd need in order to accomplish the task of raising Brent. We haven't found much yet, but we put together a small list of ingredients we'd need once we located a spell to cast. I wondered if you wouldn't be able to help me find those ingredients, or if you'd be able to point me in the right direction to locate the spell I require."

The hag drained her cup, plopped it down onto the table, and stood, her old body creaking with her jolty movements. She walked around the table until she stood next to the shelves of jars and vials and other various collections. Facing Crystal, she hummed as she lifted a gray brow. "What do you need now?"

With a smile, Crystal pulled the slip of paper from the pocket of her shorts and flattened it before she read aloud, "Death's Kiss flower petals, a dragon's talon, a skull pure of virtue, and some blood."

The hag began rustling through her jars, clouds of dust billowing up every time she moved something. Crystal wondered how she didn't continuously sneeze, breathing all that filthy air couldn't be good for her lungs. Then again, the old hag had to be quite old since she'd been an old hag when Crystal was but a child, so maybe she was doing something right within this cesspool she resided.

After a few moments, and once Logan had finished his tea as well, the hag waddled back to the table with her arms full of materials, far more than Crystal had even expected. She left that thought unsaid though as she waited for the old woman to finish scurrying around the room, apparently not yet finished.

Crystal watched while the old hag closed the distance between the table and the bookshelf in the corner, her old weathered hands shooting through cobwebs to latch onto a thick, heavy-looking book and pulling it free, dust, grime, and all. By the time she had finished, a small mound of odds and ends filled the table before Logan and Crystal.

Standing as tall as Crystal had seen her tonight, the hag

stretched and said, "Here is all but one last item, including the book..." She placed a palm on the cover of an ancient-looking text. "...containing the spell. You'll just have to retrieve that item and when you come back, bring something belonging to the dead loved one."

Crystal's mouth went dry and she swallowed down her dread.

"What do we need to retrieve?" Crystal asked, holding her breath.

"Death's Kiss flower petals."

All hope fled Crystal as she realized the task would be impossible, as no one who'd ventured near the Fields of Death had ever lived to return.

CHAPTER EIGHT

THE SPELL OF BREATHLESSNESS

CRYSTAL HAD NEVER VENTURED FURTHER south than her happy little hills. She'd never traveled any more east than the old hag's swamp. If she needed to collect the crystalized icicles from the snow-capped mountains of the north, she'd begin her trek up the jagged ridges and climb her way to the peak behind the king's castle. She would even prefer the darkest depths of the glittering lake behind the palace. Anywhere would be better than the Fields of Death south-east, where supposedly a field of flowers danced before the barren wastelands beyond.

"The army must have searched the wastelands; how did you

approach the Death's Kisses?" Crystal asked, as they rode their mounts through the forest toward the hills on which Crystal had made her home.

Logan's entire body seemed to bow inward, either from exhaustion or hopelessness, Crystal didn't know which. He gave her a sideways glance, a single lifted brow as he contemplated her question. Finally, he sighed.

"We never approached the flowers. The Sargent surmised our eventual victory rested on the shoulders of breathing men, not men consumed by the death slumber."

"But the king! Didn't he order no stone un-turned? How did you receive his approval to move on from that area without having checked the fields?"

"We lied," Logan said simply, resting his chin to his chest and hunching further.

Back to the drawing board, Crystal decided, wondering how she could succeed where an entire army had even feared trespassing. She knew the Death's Kiss was fatal to all who traveled near enough for the sweet scent to enter their senses, an intoxicating chemical that broke down a person's nervous system, leading to massive head pains, weakened muscles, memory loss, blindness, and eventual death as all organs began to shut down. Rumors had it that the flowers' intoxicating scent played with the person's mind to the point that they didn't even realize they were dying, making them not even care to escape the embrace of death.

"What if there is a way to block our sense of smell?"

Crystal pressed, not willing to give up just yet.

There had to be a way. If this ingredient was listed in a spell, then someone somewhere had used it successfully for their purposes, which meant it was possible to collect the petals of these deadly flowers. They just had to figure out how.

"You'd want to make sure that was one hundred percent effective before entering the fields, and I'm not sure how exactly you'd be able to test that theory," Logan countered. "Besides, I don't think the poison rests solely on the scent. I think it has more to do with the particles they release into the air. Once those get into your system..."

The stables and house came into view once they topped the first hill. Her clearing only a few more minutes' ride away. They rode the rest of the way in silence, their bodies aching and filthy.

Crystal dismounted near the door and led Dawn into her stall. She knew she should brush her down, but she didn't have it in her to do the task proper. Instead, she made sure the horses had fresh water and oats and promised she'd be back in the morning, after a good long sleep in the comfort of her bed, to brush down their coats and give them the love and attention they deserved.

When she glanced over at Logan in Dusk's stall, she could tell he felt the same as she watched him refill the troughs; each movement he made was as if he moved through molasses.

Crystal stopped Logan outside the stables and pointed through the space between the stables and her home. "Follow me?" she asked.

He simply nodded and motioned for her to lead the way.

She walked through the alley between her two buildings and crossed the clearing. She led him through a valley created by two large hills behind her house. As they came through the other side, she heard a sharp intake of breath from Logan as he admired the surface of the sparkling lake. It wasn't too large in size, but out here, nestled by tall hills on all sides, it was perfectly private.

Walking forward, Crystal began lifting the hem of her shirt away from her skin, pulling until it fell to the earth in a pile. She glanced over her shoulder, wearing nothing but her skirt, which she was already tugging downward, and a white lace bra.

"We're far too dirty for my poor little bathroom. Care to join me for a swim?" she said, her soft pink lips lifting into a playful smile.

He kicked his boots from his feet, hopping on one leg as he yanked his pants down. His shirt had already been stuffed into the back pocket of his jeans. He stood in nothing but his underwear, watching for what she intended.

As she walked forward, into the water, wearing nothing but her bra and panties, Logan came forward wearing nothing but his boxers.

"Why didn't you tell me of this lake before?" he asked her as they made their way further into the water.

"It must have slipped my mind," she replied, smiling over

her shoulder.

The water felt cold to her skin, but after the days they'd spent in the heat of the forest and swamp, it felt like heaven on her achy muscles. They weren't too far into fall for the water's temperature to have dropped too far yet, but it certainly felt colder than on those warm summer nights.

She didn't tread too far into the lake, preferring to stay where her feet could sink into the mud and her head could remain above the water. As Logan came closer, she roamed her hands over her body, rubbing the grime she still felt free of her skin.

She lifted her face to the sky, the sun beaming down on them from above, and ran her fingers through her knotted hair as she soaked it beneath the surface. She'd still need to bathe inside; nothing could replace how a decent bar of scented soap made her skin sing.

"Care if I do that?" Logan asked, his hands reaching forward but pausing for her consent.

"Do what?"

"I want to wash your hair," he replied.

She cocked a brow at him and then shrugged, turning her back to him. She felt the small waves his body threw her way as he closed the distance between them, and as his fingers wrapped around her now-wet tresses, she sighed at how good the gentle massage felt to her scalp.

Her tongue darted across her lips, making Logan suck in a breath as she wetted her suddenly dry mouth. He trailed his fingers through her locks, gently tugging at the knots and smoothing them free. This... this made her skin sing just as well as a scented bar of soap it seemed.

With her hair feeling less matted, she tilted her head to the side, almost unknowingly giving him better access to the sensitive skin of her neck. He needed no more encouragement than the bare skin peeking up at him as he brought his mouth down and kissed beneath her earlobe.

A sigh fell from her lips as her eyes drifted closed, and as his tongue gave her neck a different kind of massage, his hands began rubbing her sides, her back, her belly, teasing her as the tips of his fingers came tantalizingly close to her womanly areas and yet remaining too far away.

Leaning back into him, she felt how much he wanted her in this moment, and she twined her fingers up her back to unhitch her bra. His hands came up and brushed the straps down her shoulders, letting the material float beneath the surface until it disappeared, forgotten.

She moved to turn into him, but he held her firmly in place, her back pressing into his hard chest and his hands painstakingly cutting a slow, deliberate path toward her breasts. As his pruned thumb grazed her nipple, she inhaled, holding her breath as he continued to tease her with barely there touches. Her core throbbed, begging for a release of its own.

She tried to twist in his grasp again, needing to roam her hands over his body, but he held her in place. She tilted her head to peer over her shoulder, scowling with the need to get her hands on him until his mouth captured hers. She opened her mouth to protest, but his tongue met hers and released all further thoughts from her mind as she went weak in his arms.

There was nothing else, just his lips on hers, his hands agonizingly teasing her, and a passion she never thought possible.

Crystal didn't realize he'd been backing their way out of the lake until he laid her down on the grassy land surrounding the water's edge. He stood over her in nothing but a pair of drenched boxers, which showcased him and all his glory beneath the thin, dark cotton as it stuck to him. He grabbed the waistband of his underwear and raised a brow.

She sucked her bottom lip into her mouth and nodded. She watched, her eyes taking every inch of his muscular form in as he guided the material down his wet legs, releasing his arousal and making her shift.

Realizing all that stood in their way now was her own panties, she grabbed for the material, but Logan dropped himself over her, stopping her with a shake of his head. He brought his lips to hers and she gave a light nibble to his lips, making him laugh into her mouth.

The cool autumn air chilled her lake-coated skin, but as Logan brought his lips to her ear, passion warmed her, and she forgot about everything other than who she was with.

"Patience, my love," he whispered into her ear, giving her lobe a small nibble of his own as he stilled her hands.

She moaned as she shifted her hips to meet his, smiling as

his pupils dilated with need. She grazed his thick shoulders, relishing in the feel of his wet skin beneath her fingertips.

As his hand trailed down her side, sliding over her smooth, wet stomach and pinching at the fabric of her laced panties, her fingers curled into his shoulder blades and her nails left their crescent indents in the tanned skin of his back. The pain mingling with his passion had his mouth devouring hers as he pulled her underwear free, removing the only barrier left between them before he consumed every inch of her body with every inch of his.

It was three days later when Crystal found a possible solution to their dilemma. They'd closed up shop after another successful day of sales, mostly thanks to her prowess in the kitchen with her pastries and specialty coffee brews, and had headed upstairs to do some more digging into the magical texts they'd procured.

Digging into the small shipment they'd received from the travelling merchant, Crystal had settled into her seat with what she'd figured to be a fictional tale of a Necromancer on a quest to raise their sibling, who'd perished in the lake on her watch one tragic day her parents had left her in charge.

"You're not going to find anything in that book," Logan had scorned, "I'm not even sure why it's in the box."

Crystal paid him no heed. What did it really matter, at this point, if she wanted to read a story rather than research for survivable ways into the Fields of Death? They'd been trying to come up with ways to block their sense of smell to no avail. So, when she'd found the small text nestled into the bottom of the box, she'd settled into her chair, propped her feet up on the table, and began to read a sad, lonely tale of loss and guilt.

"That's it!" she had shouted, jumping from her seat and causing the chair she'd been perched on to roll backward until it clattered into the shelves behind her.

Logan startled, his entire body tensing as the pages he'd been reading flipped, and he cursed at having lost his place.

He glanced up with bloodshot eyes and she stole a peek out the window at the dark sky of night. How long had they been reading? She rubbed at her eyes, realizing how tired she was before remembering what she'd read.

"We could try what I just read!" she exclaimed, her words falling from her lips in a rush. "Monica had to find a way to bring back Beth before their parents came home, and she'd already had the dark book of spells since her mother was a dark sorcerer, but she came to the same problem we have. The damn petals. She used another spell from the dark book to give her the power to hold her breath for an extended period of time! Why don't we try that?"

She stood there; the book gripped within her tiny hands while her thumb still held her place.

A slow smile curved his lips as he stared into her emerald eyes, and he said, "Perhaps it's worth a little more research?"

"Of course! What do you take me for? It's not exactly as if I'm going to take a pinch of salt, mix it into some Dargonian berry juice, hold it to the gods and dance counter clockwise around a bonfire and say bottoms up before traipsing through the Fields of Death without first doing some research!"

She held a serious face until he cracked and laughed, causing her own giggles to spill forth.

"That's good at least," Logan finally said once the laughter had died down. Then his back straightened as he peered across the table at her. "Wait, what did that book say the spell was called?"

Crystal dragged a finger down the page, her brow wrinkled as she scoured the page for a title. She flipped back a few pages, before the naked dancing around the flickering flames, and scanned the page. Slamming her finger into the page, she exclaimed, "There! Okay, this book called it the Breathless Spell." She met his gaze again, a brow raised. "Does that sound familiar?"

"Actually..." Logan stood, closed the book he'd been reading, and made his way to one of the shelves along the wall. They had yet to collect a large number of texts, the shelves mostly bare, but he pulled a leather-bound tome from its place between two similarly bound books and brought it back to the table.

As Logan flipped through pages and scanned them for what he looked for, Crystal lifted the novel she still held and flipped back to her own page. Logan seemed to know what he was looking for, and with the hundreds of pages in the volume he currently searched, she didn't know how long it would take him to find the spell, if it had even been added to the text or not.

Leaning back in her seat again, she continued reading. She felt compelled to find out what had happened to Monica and Beth.

"A HA!" Logan screamed.

The novel Crystal had been reading fell from her grasp and hit the floor as she opened her eyes. She'd fallen asleep cramped in the chair as she was, and now her neck felt pinched as she bent to retrieve the fallen novel, placing it on the table before rubbing her eyes free of sleep.

Logan smirked at her as she righted herself in her seat, and she stuck her tongue out at him.

"On second thought," she said before rising to her feet. "I need coffee. Do you want some?"

He nodded; his head still bent over the old, thin pages as he read the page containing the spell he'd found.

She left him to it, heading down the twisting stairway and making her way into the kitchen. She stole a glance through a window on her way by and noticed it was black as pitch out there. They'd be better off staying here for the night than trying to make their way home in the dark; she didn't want to risk one of her horses becoming injured by stepping on uneven ground unknowingly.

It only took a few minutes to brew them some dark roasted

coffee. She knew how Logan drank his, with a dollop of milk only, and she added sugar cubes and a splash of milk to hers. Then she carried the over-sized mugs upstairs. She had already begun sipping hers before she even made it back to the table. These late-night research sessions were beginning to take their toll on her.

Logan took his coffee from her with a smile, tasting the steaming java before humming his approval and licking his lips.

She made her way back to her seat, pulling the chair close to the table and sitting with her back straight. Wrapping her fingers around her mug, she sighed at the warmth seeping into her fingertips, waking her even more, as she stared across the table to Logan and waited for him to share what he'd found.

"I remembered seeing this spell when I was looking through this book a few days ago, and when you were telling me about that story you were reading, about a ritual around a fire and then being able to hold their breath, it reminded me of the paintings along the edges of this spell. Do you see?"

He turned the book until she could see it right-side-up and then pushed it across the table toward her. While her fingers traced the images along the pages, he drank his coffee.

The first thing she noticed were the black-tipped white flowers. There must have been hundreds painted in intricate detail along the top corner of the page. Death's Kiss, a field of them on the thin parchment before her. Slightly below that, a small girl with hair the color of midnight stood with her head tilted high, her back to the reader, and her arms cast out to her sides horizontally while her long, dark tresses tumbled down her back. Below that image, a rippling fire burned. Her eyes flicked to the title splayed across the page: Spell of Breathlessness.

"This is it," she said, peering down the list of required ingredients. "And most of these can be found right here, in the markets!"

Logan grimaced.

"What?" she wondered aloud.

Logan leaned forward, reaching across the table and placing his index finger close to the bottom of the page.

She glanced down and read the line at which he'd pointed. *Must perform ritual beneath a full moon. Effects vary in length.* The page didn't actually specify how long the Breathlessness Spell would last though, and that tidbit of missing information could mean the death of one of them.

"We don't know how long it will last. We're going to want to bring the ritual as close to the field as we dare then. Hopefully we can get in and get out before it wears off," Crystal replied.

"And the fact that it needs to be under a full moon gives us at least a week, maybe a week and a half... I'm not entirely sure, I haven't been paying attention to the moon to be honest," Logan added.

She leaned forward and tilted her head, trying to peer through the window along the back wall to steal a glance at the moon in the sky. After twisting nearly in half, she still couldn't glimpse the damn thing. She stood and made her way to the window, stopping long enough to pick up her half drank coffee to take with her as she leaned against the wall and sipped her drink while she stared up into a cloudy sky hiding the moon from view. She sighed.

Logan pushed his chair from the table and walked over to the railing. He lay down along the edge of the loft, cushioning his head with his folded arms, and motioned for her to join him with a tick of his head. She came forward, placing her now-empty mug on the table as she passed by it, and snuggled into the crook of his arm, fitting perfectly.

"I don't think I can sleep right now, not after finishing that coffee. I should have gone for mellow roast instead," she complained, twisting in his arms to peer into his clear blue eyes.

He had a sexy as hell five o'clock shadow dusting his chin, as always, and it scratched her lightly as she brushed her cheek against it. She didn't mind the feeling though, she thought with a smile.

"I think the dark roast worked just fine," he replied, a mischievous look behind his now-hooded gaze.

She smiled. She couldn't resist the pull to him any longer, and she lost herself in his touch, his kiss, his adoring gaze. She knew eventually she'd have to figure everything out, but until then, she basked in how Logan made her feel right now instead.

They had tied their mounts a few hundred feet behind them. Crystal didn't want anything to risk her horses, not for the dark purposes of their current hike through the lands. Travelling south-east, toward the fields of flowers which could kill with just the particles in their scent, Crystal felt that luck was finally on their side as the breeze carried her hair in front of her shoulders, blowing in waves in front of her face. She spit out another clump that had flown into her mouth on the breeze.

Logan passed her a strip of cloth. When she raised an eyebrow, he stated, "For your hair."

She pulled the thread from his fingers, biting her lip to hold in her laughter at the sight of his torn button-up, red and black, short-sleeved shirt. He'd left the buttons undone, leaving her a clear glimpse at all those lovely grooves she loved trailing her tongue through. She closed her eyes and forced those thoughts away as she pulled her hair up into a loose ponytail. She'd be sad when the autumn weather turned colder as winter approached; it would steal away her glimpses of Logan, well, outside anyway.

"I think this is the last hill we should climb," Crystal said.

Her thighs throbbed with her every step, her exhaustion with this hike mounting as she pushed herself forward and up the hill. She'd never come this far south before, but from the stories she'd been told, the fact that the deep, lush green of the grass beneath their feet lightened to more of a yellow-green, she knew they were nearing the barren wastelands. She hoped that once they'd crested the hill, they'd be able to see the Fields of Death in the distance.

"Oh, wow," Logan said, his clear blue eyes flicking across the horizon.

Crystal made it up the remaining few feet and stood next to him, her gaze sweeping across the landscape of the land below them. The Fields of Death spread out as far as the eye could see along the edges of the barren wasteland. Once they made their way down the hill they'd just climbed, they'd only be about a mile away. She suddenly felt quite nervous standing up here like she was; a simple change in the wind would have her and Logan dead within minutes. They stood too close.

"Come on," she said, pulling at his hand to walk back the way they'd come.

Logan stopped her. "You're not getting cold feet, are you?"

"No." She tugged at his hand again. "I'm having a sudden attack of common sense. Let's wait for the moon down there," she said, pointing to a small leveled area partway down the hill, where if the wind did shift, they'd be safer.

With a shrug of his shoulders, Logan let himself be pulled back down the hill a piece.

Within twenty minutes, they had everything set up exactly how the spell had requested. They pulled out the few things they'd brought with them to help build a fire. Crystal hadn't known what they'd find once they made it here, and she had wanted to make sure they had come prepared.

Logan crouched low as he set the small logs into a tepee, added the kindling, and then struck the match. He had a small packet of matches within his grasp, but he'd luckily only required one. The flames began burning low, but they quickly crawled up the provided logs.

The sun had begun its slow descent as they'd pulled their supplies from their packs, and now it was only a matter of time before the moon shone bright, in all its full glory.

Crystal set to work mixing the ingredients with the mortar and pestle, crumbling the various berries and spices into a mushy powder. She'd have to wait to mix it all into the teapot until it was closer to the time she'd cast the Breathlessness Spell, but she wanted it all prepared so they didn't have to waste anymore time out here than they really needed. The field on the other side of the hill gave her chills, knowing that any hint of the flowers' scent would begin to shut her nervous system down and end her life.

"Are you ready?" Logan asked from where he lay. His sleepy gaze stared up at the stars above as he lazily watched her work between his glances up at the night sky.

"I think so," she replied, sitting next to him while she waited for the moon to climb higher.

Logan wrapped his arms around her waist and pulled her into him until he lay on his side, with her leaning against his stomach. His fingers played with her dark hair as they both watched the sky above.

The sky was clear tonight, not a cloud in sight marring the

heavens from view. If they weren't about to perform a ritual that may or may not allow them the ability to hold their breath long enough for a hike through the Fields of Death, it might have even been a romantic moment between the two of them.

Logan tucked some hair behind Crystal's ear and gently turned her chin toward him, so that her emerald eyes peered into his.

"You know I have no intention of letting you cross those fields, right?" he said, determination burning behind his steely gaze.

She pulled back from him, pinning him with a glare. "That's fine, because I don't actually have to *cross* the fields, I just have to approach them, gather some flowers, and tear free the petals for the jar," she replied, pointing to the empty jar sitting next to their nearly empty packs.

He scowled. "I mean... I'm going to go down there and get those petals. Not you."

Crystal twisted until she no longer leaned against his middle and instead sat facing where he lay curled. Her brow wrinkled. "I'm gathering the necessary ingredients to perform a necromancy spell, dark magic, yet you think I need protection from a field of flowers?"

"Deadly flowers. Yes."

She frowned. She didn't know if she wanted to pummel him for his unnecessary white knight position or throw her arms around him for caring that much about her safety. Either way, she knew she wouldn't be left behind. She wanted to raise

Brent, even if her heart felt conflicted between her undying love for Brent and this new blossoming passion between her and Logan. It was her task though, and she intended to see it through.

"I hope you realize I have no intention of being left behind," she said, playing on his own words to her moments ago.

Logan squinted at her, then held his arms out and wiggled his fingers, motioning her to his side once more.

They sat like that, pointing out shapes in the sky they'd found hiding within the stars and gasping in delight whenever they spotted a falling star. Their time for peace and games would soon come to an end as they performed the ritual that would safeguard their lives against Death's Kiss.

CHAPTER NINE

THE FIELDS OF DEATH

CRYSTAL PULLED HER JACKET FROM THE PACK ON the ground, shrugging it on and buttoning it up snug. Logan pulled his own free as well, letting it hang open over his plaid button-up shirt, which he'd finally buttoned.

As the last hour passed by, with her and Logan laughing at the shapes they'd spot, the temperatures plummeted. Shivering, Crystal approached the fire, motioning for Logan to stand on the other side of the flames, facing her.

The spell book had laid out how this was to be done, and while it could be done alone, the book made it clear that having four casters would be preferable. Crystal and Logan would make do with just the two of them; she didn't want to let anyone else know what their intentions were; the old hag, of course, being the exception.

She held the book in one hand, open to the Breathlessness Spell. Placing the book at her feet, she placed a rock on the pages to hold it open so she could read it. She picked up the small stiletto blade they'd brought and gripped it in her hand; her other hand held a glass of the juice they were going to spell. They'd already prepared the mixture, saving the last few herbs for the spell casting.

Logan held a crystal glass in one hand and a bowl of powdered herbs in the other. He nodded at her, and she dropped her gaze to the book, holding her glass to the flames as Logan held his out toward them as well.

"May the Gods above hear my plea,
May the Elements below feel my need,
May the World without taste my fee,
May the Power within know my deed."

She paused her chanting to slice the skin of her thumb, her hand still gripping the glass as she held it closer to the flames where her blood could drip into the fire.

"Grant me the ability I so seek,
Grant me the strength not to succumb to death,
Grant me the courage not to be weak,

Grant me the ability to hold my breath."

She glanced up at Logan and nodded. He threw the contents of his wooden bowl into the dancing flames, the hue of fire changing to varying shades of blue.

> "Let thy will be done,
> Let thy gifts be granted,
> Let thy power be one,
> Let thy wish be chanted."

With that, she spilled some of her juice over the blue flames and then drank the remaining contents; Logan followed suit. She gasped as the flames extinguished themselves once both glasses had been drained.

Shocked, she stepped backward as her glass shattered when it hit the ground, having slipped from her hold when her hand landed over her heart. Her heart raced as she caught Logan's gaze from across the darkened fire pit.

"Do you think the flames going out on their own means the spell worked?" Crystal asked.

Logan drew in a large breath of air, his chest puffing out almost as much as his scruffy cheeks as he pinched his lips closed. Crystal watched, trying not to laugh for fear of breaking his resolve, for several minutes. His face never turned red with the effort and he never fidgeted; he just stood there not breathing.

"Okay, okay," she said, "Let's give this a go then, shall we?"

A rush of air fell from his lips as he cut the distance between them. He gripped her by the shoulders, bringing his face inches from hers. "Please, would you just let me do this for you?"

"I can't. I have to see this through."

"I owe you my life. Let me risk mine so that you don't have to," he pleaded once more.

She cupped his face with her hands, letting her fingers play with the messy tresses of his dark brown hair. She kissed him, a soft brush of their lips together before pulling back slightly to look him in the eye.

"I love that you want to do this for me, I really do, but I *will* see this through. This is my task. I won't ask anyone to take the risks I won't take myself."

"You don't have to ask!" Logan pulled her closer still, their bodies flush.

"I said no, Logan. Now..." She stepped back, letting his hands fall from her shoulders and creating a foot of space between them. "...you can either come *with* me or wait here. That decision is yours."

Logan walked toward the dead fire pit, and Crystal tried not to feel upset that he'd chosen to stay behind. Her eyes widened as he bent to scoop up the glass jar. He held it firmly as he walked toward her, holding his free hand out to her. She smiled, grasping onto his hold and entwining their fingers together before they climbed the hill.

Before they crested the top, Logan turned toward Crystal, stopping their forward momentum. He lifted his hand to brush some of the hair that had fallen from her loose ponytail aside, but he held onto a few tendrils instead, twisting the strands between his fingers as he stared into her eyes.

The moon cast his face in shadows, providing enough light to see but softening the sharp edges shown beneath the sun's bright rays. It made him handsomer, dreamier, beneath the soft glow.

"Before we get any closer and have to start holding our breaths, I wanted to say something in case I don't have another chance," he said, his voice low and heated with passion.

She held a finger to his lips, hushing his goodbyes. Shaking her head, she said, "No, Logan. Please don't. I don't want to hear your goodbye. Nothing is going to happen to us. We're going to go gather what we need, and then we're going to get far, far away from here. We don't need to say goodbyes."

Logan scowled, a half grin lifting his lips as he brushed away her hand from his mouth, his other hand still at his side with the empty jar held tight. "Would you just let me talk, you stubborn woman!" he scolded in a light tone. "You won't let me take the risk; you can damn well let me tell you I love you before we approach the Fields of Death!"

Crystal's mouth dropped, and she held her hands over her mouth. She'd known he was falling for her; in fact, she felt confident that she, too, was falling for him. It didn't make any of this easier though. She felt the need to see this quest through, to raise Brent. She owed him that much at least. Didn't she?

But Logan had never pronounced his love of her aloud before, and having the words hang in the air between them, with him staring into her eyes as if he wanted to devour every inch of her skin atop this moonlit hill with nothing but his lips, made her realize something else. She wasn't just *falling* for Logan; she'd already fallen. That thought didn't bring her any comfort; it made her actions even more conflicting.

"I think I love you too, but it just makes everything so confusing," she replied. She chewed her bottom lip as she stared into his loving gaze.

He trailed his fingers along the curve of her jaw, brushing his thumb over her dainty chin. He smiled knowingly down at her before he pressed his lips to her forehead in a chaste kiss. "I know this isn't easy, and I know I've muddled the line drawn in the sand between us, but none of it has to matter. I gave you my word that I would help you with this task. Come on, we can figure all of this out later. Let's get down there before the effects of the spell have a chance to wear off."

She nodded, feeling colder when he pulled his hand from her face. Looking into each other's eyes, they gasped in a large breath of air, puffing their cheeks with the effort, and turned toward the Fields of Death below.

It didn't take them long to make it down the hill. The whole not breathing thing seemed to be the biggest difficulty they faced, as it was something done naturally. Crystal had let out air a few times, and Logan had nudged her each time as a gentle reminder not to breathe.

The field was a good twenty minutes from the bottom of the hill, but the even ground they traversed made it easier for them to hold their breath. They walked hand in hand until they made it close enough to the flowers that they could stop and approach the field with precaution.

Just the scent of these beautiful flowers caused devastating effects that eventually led to death. As Crystal knelt before the field, the Death's Kiss flowers within her reach, Logan nudged her again, causing her to glance up to where he stood. He ripped more cloth from his red and black plaid button up, closing his jacket again after he handed her the larger square of fabric.

When she raised a brow at him, he pointed to his hands and mouthed, 'Don't let them touch your skin.' She nodded her understanding and then turned, using the fabric he'd given her to pluck several stems from the ground.

Once she had a deadly bouquet gripped within her palm, making sure to keep the cloth between the stems and her skin at all times, she stood and tilted her head toward the hill they'd crested to make their way to the fields.

He nodded, still holding the glass jar within his grasp, and walked side-by-side with her until they weren't so close to the Fields of Death.

Crystal fell to her knees, dropping the flowers to the ground.

She used the cloth to pull the petals free, dropping them one by one into the open jar Logan had placed on the ground before her. She used precise movements, careful not to let the petals, stems, or any parts of the flowers touch the outside of the jar. It would do no one any good if the residue coated the glass they intended to carry.

A pain wrenched from her chest, and she dropped her hold on the cloth, letting the flowers fall to the ground. She glanced up at Logan, who stood looking down on her with confusion creasing his brow. Her lungs constricted, and some of her breath wheezed past her lips. Her eyes widened as she stood.

'What?' Logan mouthed, concern pinching his lips.

Crystal's hands flew to her throat, her eyes watering with the strain her lungs felt.

Realization dawned across Logan's face and he stepped right up to her. He pulled her face to his, covered her lips with his own, and expelled some of the breath he'd been holding into her mouth. She gasped it in greedily before he pulled away, too soon. He pointed frantically up the hill, and as she turned to bolt up the hill and away from the field below, she watched Logan kneel to gather the petals himself from over her shoulder as she ran.

She didn't make it to the top of the hill before she collapsed. Her legs felt like soggy bread, no longer willing to support her weight. Her fingers dug into the soil, pulling her farther away from the fields below as she held the breath Logan had shared.

As her arm slammed down on the ground near the top of the

hill, her vision narrowed until only the darkness remained.

When Crystal's eyes fluttered open, she found herself lying next to their burnt-out fire on the small landing on which they'd waited to perform their ritual. Logan's arms held her close, her upper body draped over his folded knees as he cradled her to him. The small jar sat, filled with black tipped white petals, just a short distance away from them. He'd finished the task without her, and he'd brought her farther away from the Fields of Death.

"How long have I been out for?" she asked, her voice scratchy. She raised her gaze to the sky, but she couldn't tell how long the sun would be from rising. She hadn't mastered the art of star-reading.

"Not long," Logan said, grazing her cheek with the back of his hand. He stared down into her eyes, not looking away, not blinking, just watching her as she watched him. "You gave me quite the scare," he said finally, bringing his lips to her forehead.

"What happened?"

She remembered plucking the petals from the flowers, using Logan's shirt to protect her skin. She remembered feeling as though she were drowning, the pressure building and building. Logan's lips had met hers, sharing what little breath he had held, but it hadn't been enough. She hadn't run fast enough, far enough. The rest was still a blur.

"The spell didn't last long enough for you. You ran out of air too soon. I finished the task as quickly as possible, and when I climbed the hill to return to you, I found you unconscious near the top of the hill. I brought you here because I knew it was safer than leaving you there. Those damned flowers scare the crap out of me," he explained, his fingers still dancing across the skin of her face.

Feeling stronger, she sat up straighter. She pulled the fabric from her hair, loosening her locks down her back in waves, and ran her fingers through the strands to fix some of the chaos. Logan watched as she tied the string back into her hair, pulling it back up into a ponytail.

She leaned forward, reaching for the jar containing the deadly petals, and held it up to her face. They looked so harmless, beautiful even. They would probably look amazing in a center piece.

With the final ingredient in her grasp, she realized she had everything she needed to raise Brent from the dead. She and Logan had done it! She gave him a sideways glance, noticing the smile he had while watching her movements, and held the jar up.

"We did it, Logan! We really did it!" she squealed, dropping the jar back to the grass and tackling Logan.

Her arms wrapped around his neck as she rolled on top of him. Her dark locks hung down one side of her face, swinging from where she had tied it. Her body pressed into his as she held her head above his by leaning on her elbows. Her emerald green eyes glittered with glee as she stared down into his face, her gaze dropping to his charming smirk. She dragged her tongue across her lips, wetting them.

His hands shot up, grabbed her head, and pulled her down to him, kissing her with a passion that demanded to be fed.

Her lips parted on a sigh, and his tongue dove forward, mingling with hers in a seductive give and take dance. She moaned into his mouth, feeling his arousal awaken beneath her. She pulled away from his kiss, straddling him as she sat straight above him.

Her fingers grazed a line down his chest, flicking at the buttons one-by-one. With a mischievous grin, she tugged with both hands, popping the buttons free and displaying his defined chest. The moonlight above basked him in a magical glow, and she brought her mouth down to kiss the skin she'd revealed.

A screech released from her throat as Logan flipped her to her back, and she giggled as he now straddled her. He brought his scruffy chin to her neck, tickling her with his unshaven beard before teasing her sensitive skin with kisses. He pulled her earlobe into his mouth, sucking gently before trailing kisses down her neck, to her chest. He sat up, staring down at her with a grin full of mischief.

"Don't you dare," she scolded, reaching for his hands.

He swatted her reach away and gripped her t-shirt between two hands and pulled, a loud tear sounding through the night.

Crystal threw her head back and laughed.

Logan brought his kisses lower, making her blood scream for more. She loved the feel of him atop her; the attention his mouth gave to her every whim. The cold air of the night couldn't chill the heat they built with one another, not as their passions soared and their love grew.

With the jar of Death's Kiss petals an arm's reach away, the last ingredient necessary to raise her dead lover, Crystal lost herself in the arms of the man who was still very much alive. His every touch igniting her soul to their connection, making her feel more alive now than she had ever felt in her entire lifetime.

And as Logan brought her to release, her ecstasy left her more confused than ever about what would come next.

CHAPTER TEN

THE RAISING OF A LIE

THE NEXT DAY, AFTER CLOSING THEIR SHOP AND hanging a sign in the window to let their customers know they'd be re-opening the shop next week, giving them a few days reprieve to bring the old hag the jar of petals, Crystal and Logan traveled back to her cozy home in the hills. They kept quiet most of the way, a blanket of discomfort settling over them at the prospect of what they'd soon be attempting. Crystal felt obligated to see this quest through, but she also felt conflicted.

Looking next to her, she watched Logan scratching Dusk's neck in the stall next to hers as she brushed Dawn's coat with care. A routine the two of them had maintained since they'd opened their small shop in town. Watching him move around Dusk though, Crystal knew the two of them could be happy growing old together, and Brent had been gone so long, she really didn't know if that would be possible in quite the way she *knew* Logan and her would manage.

As memories of Logan filled her heart, the ones of Brent seemed almost faded. It was as if she saw those loving moments between the two of them through the reflection off a foggy glass.

Logan looked up, catching her as she stared at him, her teeth chewing her bottom lip while she was lost in thought. He smiled across the stables at her, then bent his head back down to his task.

The love he felt for her hung thick in the air; the happy carefree mood of the horses made her believe even they could feel it. It wrapped around her and warmed her soul. Had she ever felt this way with Brent?

They finished with the horses and left them to their oats, climbing the veranda into her own home a short distance away a few moments later. Logan went straight to the kitchen to throw on a pot of tea, and Crystal went around the main floor lighting the candles and torches; she preferred the natural glow of a flickering flame over the electric glow of fluorescent light bulbs and used the candles and torches whenever she could.

She pulled the book from the shelf, the one in which she'd found the hint for the Breathlessness Spell, and settled down in one of the chairs angled toward the stone fireplace.

A few minutes later, she'd already finished the chapter she'd started before leaving that morning for work, and Logan set two teacups down on the small, rounded table nestled between the two chairs. He knelt in front of the fireplace, pulling a box of matches from his trousers' pocket and lit the logs. Sitting down next to her, he lifted his cup to his lips and sipped.

"Do you want to talk about what's been bothering you all day?" he asked as he placed his cup down, his gaze resting on the dancing flames in front of them.

Once they'd made it home last night from the Fields of Death, Crystal and Logan had spent the night together in her bed. She never felt confused when Logan held her or loved her. The entire night had passed with them showing each other how much they cared for one another. Brent hadn't crossed her mind once. Whenever they were not taking full advantage of each other's bodies, that's when the doubt crept in, paralyzing her with a fear she didn't expect. What if she chose wrong?

She dropped the book to her lap, laying it open to her spot and resting her hand in the crook between pages. With her free hand, she reached for her cup, blowing on it to cool it before sipping some of the sweetened tea. She licked her lips as she set the cup down, and then she sighed as she turned to face Logan.

It wasn't fair not to tell him what was on her mind. At least not when it concerned him as well. He'd told her how he felt, where he stood, and he'd left it up to her to decide, making sure she knew he'd be with her until the end. He wanted her, but if it ended when they raised Brent, he had accepted that.

The problem now was that she wanted them both. She loved Logan, and these past several weeks had been like living in a fantasy tale. But she remembered loving Brent too. She had waited months for his return, had searched for him in a sick house, and then had vowed to bring him back from the grave. Those weren't actions someone would commit themselves to without having loved that person, were they?

"I'm more confused than ever about what to do," she blurted, watching him where he sat next to her in order to gauge his reaction.

He kept his face straight, pressing his lips together in that way of his when he contemplated things. He rubbed a hand along the bottom of his jaw before replying, "I haven't made things less confusing, have I?"

She smiled. "No, you really haven't."

Stretching a hand across the space between their chairs, Logan brushed his fingertips along the skin of her forearm. Her gaze dropped to his loving touch; her heart already singing for more. "Do you want me to stop?"

"Yes. No." She groaned, lifting her hand to rub her temples and dropping his fingers from her arm. "I don't know." She sighed, her shoulders drooping as her confusion mounted higher still.

Logan rose from his seat and knelt before her, pulling her

hand into his while staring into her emerald green eyes.

She looked down at him, a crease in her brow as she tried to figure out what he was doing. The only thought screaming through her head was: *He better not be doing what I think he's doing!*

"Crystal, you know how I feel for you. You know that I am here for you no matter what. I gave you my word that I would see this through, and I still mean that. Even if it means I lose you to Brent. He will be one lucky bastard, and I might silently curse his name whenever I pass him on the street, but if he is what will make you feel whole, happy, and content, then I want that for you. Why don't we take the stress out of this and finish what we started? I don't think you'll be able to decide until the deed is done. Okay?"

She nodded. He was probably right anyway. They'd been preparing for this spell for weeks, and the entire time they'd been doing so, she'd been confused. Nothing seemed to sway her decision fully one way or the other.

Crystal lifted her hand from his grasp and cupped his cheek, her thumb running over the dark scruff of his unshaven face. A tear slipped from her eye at the words he'd spoken. The relief she felt was like a weight off her shoulders, and she could breathe again. A smile tugged at her lips as she held his gaze.

"You're right. I don't have to worry about it right now. I can wait until we've performed the spell that will bring him back. I can save his life and then decide. If I stay with you," she said, brushing her thumb over his bottom lip as she wet her own, "then at least we've saved his life."

"Exactly," Logan replied.

Raising himself higher, Logan brought his lips to hers. He then climbed to his feet and returned to his seat, picking up his own book, something about kings and dragons, and began to read.

They sat like that for hours, just silently reading together. Then they went to their separate bedrooms, knowing they needed a good night's rest before the tasks of tomorrow.

They approached the worn-down hut with caution, half-waiting for the old hag to fly out her creaky door with a broom waving around in her angry, wrinkled fist. When they made it to the porch without incident, Crystal rapped twice on the ancient-looking screen door. She bit her lip, stifling her laughter, at the mumbling she could hear coming toward her from the other side of the door. Logan covered his own amusement with an awkward cough.

The heavy, inside door banged open and the old hag scowled through the screen at them. Seeing it was them, her creased brow deepened as she huffed before waving them inside. She backed away, giving them room to enter, and mumbled curses under her breath as they came in and closed the door behind themselves.

The old hag wore another too-large dress that hung from her

thick form in tatters, and Crystal's nose twitched at the stench filling the small space. It would do this place wonders if the old woman would just open her windows from time to time; though, perhaps the surrounding swap would make even that ineffective.

"We brought the final ingredient, and..." Crystal dug through the pockets of her thin, white, fluttering skirts. "...I brought this as well. It belonged to Brent. Well, it belonged to his father and he and his brother fought over it, but it was him who inherited it."

The small, old-fashioned pocket watch dangled from the tiny links of its chain between them, but she pulled it back toward herself when the hag reached for it.

The hag raised a brow.

"Will you help us perform the spell?"

The swamp witch waved a hand, annoyed. "I already said I would, didn't I, child?" her scratchy voice scolded as she held her palm open again. This time, Crystal dropped the pocket watch into her crinkled hold.

Crystal watched as the old woman held Brent's watch to her face, crossing the room to one of her shelves and picking up a round circle of magnifying glass. She shoved the glass into her eye, scrunching her weathered face to hold it into place as she brought the watch closer still. Inspecting it for what, Crystal didn't know.

"And the petals? You found a way to collect some Death's Kiss?" she asked, placing the watch onto the cluttered table after shoving a mess of papers, trinkets, and vials aside.

Logan stepped forward, pulling the jar from the pack hanging at his hip. He placed it next to the watch on the table and stepped back to Crystal's side.

The witch immediately grabbed for the jar, her eyes alight with excitement. Her fingers danced along the glass, almost as if she was attempting to count the individual petals. She glanced up at them then, her tongue darting between her missing teeth to wet her lips.

"I'll help you cast your spell, but for a price," the hag finally said.

Anger welled inside of Crystal. If the witch wanted to charge them a fee for her aid, then she should have specified that beforehand. Now they'd have to make another trip through the swamp to cast the spell and raise Brent. Crystal had wanted to get that over with now so she could move forward with her life, with whatever man she should choose.

"Why didn't you mention a cost before now?" Crystal asked, her tone akin to a growling lion as she gritted her teeth.

The old hag's mouth dropped open before she snapped it shut with a smile. She set the jar down on the table again and waved her hands in front of her while she shook her head. "Oh no, no, no! You misunderstood me, dear." She pointed at the jar. "There are more than enough petals for your spell to work. I simply wanted to ask for the remaining Death's Kiss for my own concoctions afterward."

Crystal relaxed. "I don't see why not. It's not as if I'll need them."

"Good." The hag clapped her hands before making her way to the bookshelf and pulling the same volume they'd been perusing their last visit. "Then let's get started, shall we? We'll want to wait for the sun to fall. Raising the dead is a task best left for the shadows."

Crystal and Logan drank cups of coffee spiked with some of the old hag's own concoction of liquor. Crystal didn't know what blend had been used, but it tasted strong enough to wake the dead, which seemed fitting enough for their current situation.

Logan talked about funny customers he'd met since opening their shop, about the strange things he'd seen during his time soldiering, and his desires to own a dog at some point in his future. Crystal appreciated the distraction, and she knew he filled her mind with these off-topic stories to ease her anxieties of the task before them. Once they'd raised Brent, she'd have to decide with who she wanted to spend her future.

The swamp witch busied herself mixing some foul smelling brew in a cast iron cauldron set up in the kitchen over a hearth, leaving the two to their privacy for the most part. She mumbled to herself under her breath almost constantly, creating a hum of chaos wherever she wobbled. Her wide hips had knocked Crystal's chair a few times as she'd pass by with more ingredients in her hands to drop into the potion she brewed, the spell book open on the countertop next to her.

After a while, when the sun had long since fallen, Crystal

spoke up.

"Exactly how dark do these shadows need to be?"

The hag peered across the room at her, poking her head out of the kitchen doorway. She scowled, shaking a wooden spoon at her impatience. "These things take as long as they take. If you want to make yourselves useful, take that pocket watch and grab a dagger from that shelf and head outside. Around back, you'll see my caster's circle." Then the hag disappeared into the kitchen again, clattering dishes as she worked.

Picking up the watch from the table, Crystal let it dangle from her grasp as she stood. Logan beat her to the shelf and picked a dagger from the small selection at random. She followed him through the front door and out into the swamp.

For once, the stench of the bog didn't seem nearly as bad. Whatever concoction the hag had been brewing, Crystal hoped drinking it was not on the agenda for tonight.

Walking around the side of the house, Crystal stayed close to Logan. Without the sun to guide them, they had only the flickering flames held within torches inside of the house, which cast only a slight glow through each window. Perhaps if the glass had been cleaned anytime within this decade, they'd have had more light to go on, but the hag didn't seem to mind the filth.

A short distance behind the hut, Crystal found the clearing the hag had mentioned. A brick path slowly formed beneath their feet as they walked, and with each forward step, the pathway seemed to climb until they made their way up a few steps and stood atop a circular platform made of interlocking gray and green bricks. At least they'd escaped the suctioning mud for a small bit.

They only waited a few minutes before the hag banged her way through a back door Crystal hadn't recognized from within the rundown hut. She carried a smaller cauldron toward them, the stench immediately making Crystal's nose wrinkle.

As the witch walked past her and set the pot down in the center of the circle, Crystal noticed the foul liquid inside for the first time. A slop of gray goo filled the pot, bubbling slowly in a tar like manner. She had to breathe through her mouth to prevent herself from getting sick, and she would swear she could even taste the stench upon her tongue.

"Please tell me we don't have to consume that," Logan asked, his nose covered with his t-shirt.

"Don't be daft! This is to be spilled within the circle. Since we don't have Brent's grave dirt, or his grave, we'll need a magical barrier in which he can cross the realms of life and death. This will open that barrier, and I will hold the key to those who wish to cross. We can't have just anyone pushing into life, can we?" She cackled, amused with herself it seemed.

The hag left them and returned to the house. Several minutes later, she returned with the book of spells and a roll of bandages. Crystal bit her lip, her anxiety rising as the time to raise Brent rushed closer.

The witch placed the roll into Logan's hand, a crinkle around her eyes as she held his hand with the bandages and studied him. With a nod, she guided him to a spot near the steps to the dais, behind Crystal. She relieved him of the dagger and left him there.

She passed the dagger to Crystal and then crossed the circle to the cauldron.

"Are you ready?"

Crystal swallowed her fear. "Yes."

The old hag lifted the black cauldron and poured its contents onto the bricks. She walked around the spillage in a circle, filling in the spaces until a large enough area had been covered. Brent would have more than enough room to escape whatever afterlife within which he'd been captured.

Once the cauldron had been placed on the stairs, the old woman moved to stand across the circle from Crystal. Her hands shot into the air, and she started shouting words Crystal couldn't decipher. A language she'd never heard in her lifetime.

The thought screamed across her mind that this spell could be anything, and without her being able to understand the words spoken, how could she be one hundred percent sure the hag's intentions matched her own?

The wind began to pick up, howling through the broken limbs of the trees surrounding the old hag's hut. The night seemed to darken as clouds rushed in, stealing the moon's glow intermittently. As the hag screamed her incantations, lightning flashed across the sky. Crystal couldn't be sure the spell being cast was the one she had asked, but she could certainly tell it was dark magic being worked.

"You must use the blade now; a price must be paid. You'll pay with your blood, and you'll coat the object belonging to the loved one you wish to retrieve from the dark lord's realm of death."

Crystal's hair whipped around her face as the storm grew around them. She fixed the old hag with a hard stare. Did she trust this woman? Was she about to get sacrificed? Did that work this way?

She didn't know, and now she felt like a fool for not doing more research before rushing over here to perform this ritual.

As the old hag raised a brow at her, she decided to just go with it. They'd come too far to back out now. She sent a silent prayer to her maker for safe passage should this be her end.

Then, gritting her teeth, she held the chain of the pocket watch in the same hand with which she gripped the blade, her other hand clasped around the hilt. She drew in a deep breath, closed her eyes, and sliced the skin of her palm in one quick motion. Air rushed through her teeth as the blade bit into her skin, and she grimaced as she held her hand over the gray-green sludge that would become the entrance between realms. Her blood fell from her closed fist, coating Brent's watch and falling to the ground.

As the first drops hit the mixture coating the ground, blinding light flashed from the circle, stealing Crystal's ability to see. The swamp witch howled more incantations into the night, the wind blowing with a force that nearly knocked

Crystal from her feet.

When Crystal's vision cleared, she gasped as dark tendrils of smoke began to waft from the ground before her. She pulled her hand away from the lifting haze, letting her bloody hand fall to her side.

The old hag screeched, her hands whipping through the air until she fell to her knees, her fingers splayed within the muck she'd brewed as she continued chanting in the language unknown.

Crystal's eyes widened as the smoke fell beneath the sludge, disappearing from view as the storm raging around them died. The silence sent a chill down Crystal's spine as she glared across the circle to where the witch now knelt.

The brewed potion turned to dust before her eyes, blowing away on the slight breeze they'd stepped out into earlier, and Crystal scowled.

"Where is he?" she bit out, her anger almost palpable between them.

She'd come a long way not to have her lover returned to her, and she no longer believed the hag had performed the right ritual at all.

The swamp witch rose to her feet, brushing dust from her fingers and the dingy fabric of her skirts as she straightened. She crossed the now empty circle, stopping in front of where Crystal stood with her arms crossed over her chest, her bloody fist already dried with the caked-on blood.

Jabbing a finger into Crystal's chest twice, the witch

growled out, "If you want to raise the dead, you should make sure they're actually dead first."

Shoving past her, Crystal stood there for a moment, confused. When she came back to her senses, she turned on her heel and stormed past where Logan stood dumbfounded. She grabbed the hag by the shoulder and turned her around.

"What do you mean: make sure they're dead first?" she asked. The thoughts whirling around her head couldn't possibly be true.

The witch grabbed the dagger from Crystal's hand. "Exactly how it sounds. Brent isn't in the realm of the dead."

CHAPTER ELEVEN

THE SPELL OF FINDING

LOGAN AND CRYSTAL WERE BACK IN THEIR BOOK shop the very next day. They'd spent the night in an awkward slumber hunched over the old hag's table in the main room, and when they'd left, the hag had ripped two pages from her spell book and sent them on their way, scowling and scolding that Crystal's next visit better not come anytime soon. Privacy, that's what had placed the hag in the swamp and she'd made it clear she'd continue to enjoy it once they'd stopped calling on her for favors, especially if they were going to make her go through all of the trouble of raising the dead when there was no dead to raise.

Crystal hadn't slept well that night, and they'd only stopped at their house on the hills long enough to change out of their swamp-stenched clothing. She hadn't realized when she'd started calling her cozy house theirs either, but that was just another thought jumbled in her confused head at the moment.

Once they had opened the store, Crystal busied herself in the kitchen all day. Baking chocolate treats and feeding her soul with the sinfully delicious snacks. She drank enough coffee to keep the entire town awake for three days, but she didn't care. She knew once they turned their open sign around that she'd be consumed with the thoughts that had kept her awake most of the night prior.

Logan hadn't said much to her as they'd ridden from the swamp. In fact, he'd stayed silent most of the day as well. She didn't know what he thought of all of this. She'd dragged him through all this insanity, and last night, when it was supposed to all be over one way or the other, they ended up face to face with an entirely different outcome; one Crystal hadn't even fathomed existed. Brent wouldn't have just left her waiting knowingly. There had to be another reason for his absence.

At the end of the day, when there were only a few hours of daylight left, Logan flipped their open sign around, closing the store to further patrons. Crystal passed Logan a mug of coffee, and while he raised a brow at her next cup of java, he never said a thing.

She took the spiral stairs and set her cup down at the spot in which she'd spent many evenings studying. Then she pulled the now somewhat crumpled pages from her pocket and flattened them out in front of her on the long table as Logan took a seat across from her with his own cup of coffee.

She hadn't really looked too much into the pages the swamp witch had parted with, only glancing down at the titles written across the tops of each long enough to notice they were different spells. Now, as she looked down at them, she realized one of them was the Grave Dirt Necromancy Spell, which could be performed around the grave of the one you wished to resurrect, on the back of that page was a Death Curse, which seemed entirely too easy to cast for Crystal's peace of mind, and the other spell seemed to be a fairly simple Seek and Find Spell.

Logan leaned over the table, peering at the words on the pages for a moment before sitting back and casually drinking his coffee. The silence he found easy began to anger Crystal. They had been on this quest together since she'd helped nurse Logan's burns from his skin; he didn't even have any burns or scars, an effect that wouldn't have been possible without her risking a trip through the swamps to seek out the hag she hadn't spoken to in years. Now that they'd found answers they hadn't been seeking, he seemed to be a closed book, and Crystal had had enough.

"Why are you so quiet?" she asked, her eyes reading what she could from him.

He sat slouched in his seat, sipping the coffee she'd made for him. When his eyes met hers, there was a darkness brooding behind his usually light blue irises. She chewed her lip, realizing his silence masked his hurt.

"I want to give you whatever time you need to process what happened last night. I'm still here with you, whatever you decide."

"Whatever I decide?"

"You have a few options at your disposal now," he replied simply, drinking more of his coffee as a distraction.

She supposed he was right, and she realized she admired the fact that he kept silent in order not to sway her decision. Though, that realization only added to the difficult choices she had before her. She had the Spell of Finding at her fingertips, literally, and she could hunt down Brent and rescue him from whatever had kept him from her. Logan would probably offer his aid, but could she really ask him to go through all that trouble for her lover?

Or... Crystal could leave Brent where he was and live her life happy, surrounded by Logan's love. A thought that made her heart swell with possibilities. She knew they'd grow old together happily, running this shop they'd started until they were an old scraggily couple. They'd probably have a few kids, maybe a dog. Her life would be full of love. But could she do that?

Crystal's gaze met Logan's, and Logan released a sigh, leaning forward to tap the page on the table. "So, we're going to try the Search and Find Spell?" he asked.

Her shoulders drooped and she nodded. "I have to see this

through. What if he's in trouble?"

He smiled, his eyes lighting up at her statement. "That's another reason why I love you," he said, making her heart beat a little faster with his proclamation. "You persevere no matter what. You're the most determined woman I have ever met. And you won't give up until you know what's happened. Here," he said, nodding toward the spell between them, "let me see that."

Crystal passed the spell across to him and sat back with her coffee while his eyes scanned the page. She wondered about the woman who had captured Logan's heart before he'd set off to fight the king's war. They never talked much about her, and Crystal didn't press him to either. Now, though, she couldn't help but be curious who she had been. She apparently wasn't as determined as Crystal was, but with all the fine qualities she'd come to love of Logan's, she knew the woman must have been something special.

"This actually looks fairly eas—What are you looking at?" he said as he realized she stared across the table at him, unblinking and lost in thought.

"What you said, it made me think of what came before the war for you," she replied, her voice quiet, unsure.

Logan's gaze dropped to the table and a shadow fell over his features.

She wished she'd kept her mouth shut; wished she didn't bring forth Logan's own memories of a painful past. Curiosity had killed the mood in this room, but no more than Brent's unknown whereabouts had.

Finally, he looked up; a far-off look of love shining through his hooded gaze.

"Angela, you remind me so much of her sometimes. You both look nothing alike, but you both hold the fiercest personalities in your petite forms. She was wild and carefree; she'd do whatever popped into her mind without restraint. When she loved, she loved with every fiber of her being. I swear, just being in our empty home while she had gone to market, you could feel the love consuming you from the very walls, as if the house itself had learned to breathe love. And when she'd found out she was carrying our child; she'd filled our lives with planning for our bundle of joy's arrival."

He dropped his gaze to his clasped fists on the tabletop, a darkness crossing his eyes once more.

"It's okay," Crystal interrupted him. "You don't have to tell me anymore."

Logan quirked his lips into a half grin and reached across the table, the spell forgotten between them as he gave her small hands a squeeze and held onto them. She couldn't believe his actions, that he'd comforted her when his own heart must have been shattering inside his rib cage again with the memories she'd brought back to his attention.

"I loved Angela, with my whole heart. I loved her when I'd been conscripted. I loved her when I fought through the wars. And I almost died happily at that sick house, knowing I'd be reunited with her and our child. But when you waltzed into that room and wrenched those curtains open and stood by my side as I healed, I began to realize I hadn't been gifted with just one love." He squeezed her hands again. "I'd been given two."

A tear slipped down Crystal's cheek at the love she felt. She could feel how he'd felt for Angela; she knew the love they'd shared had been right out of a fairy tale, and she could feel how much he cared for her in this moment, too. It had been their grief that had brought them together, forging a love stronger than either of their last relationships. And in this moment, Crystal knew what she would do with their futures.

"I'm choosing you, Logan. This is the life I want. I want to run this little shop with you for the rest of our lives. I want to go home with you every night. And I want you to be the first person I see when I wake each day. I want our life," she said in a rush.

"What does that mean about this?" Logan asked, pointing at the spell still on the table between them with his elbow, not letting go of her hands.

"If you'll still help me, I'd like to search for Brent. I need to know why he never returned; he might need my help."

Logan nodded. "I will always help you. The good thing is," he said, dropping her hands to bring the spell to her attention, "this spell only requires something belonging to the person you seek, and for you to chant these words repeatedly. Supposedly, the item will lead you in the direction of who you wish to find."

"When should we do this? Does it matter when?"

"It doesn't specify a time or moon cycle. Why don't we keep the shop closed tomorrow and begin at first light?"

She smiled. "That sounds perfect! I can't wait to put this all behind us and begin our lives together."

Logan's hands brushed the skin of her stomach, the tips grazing her breasts, teasing. She stretched, yawning awake and smiling at him as he furthered the exploration of her body.

They'd fallen into bed together last night once they'd finished at the shop, and they'd both been too exhausted for anything other than catching up on some of the missing slumber from the prior few days.

His busy fingers now trailed across her skin, barely grazing her at all but sending her blood rushing through her veins begging for more.

She rolled into his side, draping a bare leg over his as she wrapped her arms around his neck and pulled him in for a kiss. She could get used to waking up like this.

His breath smelled, and his tongue tasted of old coffee, but she drove those away with her own morning mouth kisses, and neither one of them seemed to mind. She trailed her fingers down his naked chest, twirling them around his nipples before she flicked her tongue over each.

He chuckled, gripping her by the shoulders and flipping her around until she lay beneath him on her back. He mounted her, pinning her under his weight as he held her wrists by her head with one hand. She bit her lip at the thought of being at his mercy, and his Adam's apple bobbed as he swallowed, his erection gaining confidence through his boxers just from the sight of her.

"I want to show you how much I adore you," he said, his voice thick with the passion he felt.

She nodded her consent and gasped as he brought his mouth down to her neck, pulling her nightgown up and over her head between his kisses and using the bunched-up material to further restrain her wrists. Her tongue darted out to wet her lips as his teeth teased her nipple, and as he clamped down slightly, sending a shiver of pain to mingle with her lust, she moaned and shifted her hips.

He continued his torture of gentle pain mixed with barely there touches, even his breath on her moistened flesh from his kisses was a sweet kind of torture. He pulled his boxers off at some point, she didn't know when, and the feel of his skin meeting hers nearly drove her wild.

She couldn't take his teasing for much longer, and her breathing came faster and faster as she wriggled her hands, wanting to pull him to her.

"Please," she begged, making him smile.

Releasing his hold on her hands, he positioned himself above her, and as he prepared to make her scream his name, she clutched at him as if the thought of being apart were too much to bear.

He loved her then, showing her he'd love her always, and as she tumbled over the edge of release, she knew she'd never grow tired of his arms around her or his love within her. He was her home.

It took them nearly an hour to gain the strength to leave their bed behind. Crystal made her way to the kitchen, wishing to pack a small sack of supplies for their trip and making breakfast before they departed, while Logan hurried off to the stables to ready their horses. There was no telling how far they'd have to travel to locate Brent.

After they sat and ate a small breakfast of strawberry jammed toast and finished their mugs of coffee, they set off. Logan bundled the small pack of supplies into Dusk's saddlebag, while Dawn had survival supplies already bundled into hers; a tent, some gear for a fire, and cooking and hunting supplies.

Once Crystal sat atop Dawn, with Logan and Dusk next to her, she pulled the crinkled paper containing the Find and Seek Spell from her pocket. She glanced at Logan, who gave her a reassuring grin, and then she dug into her other pocket to retrieve the pocket watch still stained with her blood. Dangling the chain in front of her, her other hand gripping the spell and the saddle horn, she began to chant.

"Seekers seek and finders find,
This item belongs to the one I seek.
Use thy sight to aid my bind,

And grant thy caster a telling peek."

The pocket watch seemed to pull westward, swaying on the chain as she continued to chant beneath her breath. With a quick glance at Logan, they began trotting west, following the direction the watch tugged.

They had to stop every twenty minutes or so, waiting for Crystal to chant the spell again to check they were still heading in the correct direction. The watch continued to lead their way, but it quickly became clear they were headed nowhere near Dargonia.

"What's west of Dargonia?" Crystal asked, leading her horse through a small creek.

She didn't know the surrounding land all that well, having lived most of her life in Dargonia. She knew her hills, she knew the swamp, and she knew the town itself. Other than that, she wasn't well traveled, never straying too far from the places she knew.

Logan was a soldier though, and he'd fought through the dark wars against the sorcerers. Those battles alone would have led him across the lands; he'd even shared stories of towering castles, darkened caverns, and overgrown islands filled with secrecy and darkness. He'd know better than she what was west.

"There's a small farming village not far from where we are. Daxonville. We might even be able to make it there before nightfall if the watch doesn't lead us in another direction before then," he replied, keeping his horse close to hers. If she wanted to, she could reach out and hold his hand, if she didn't already hold the spell and pocket watch within her grip.

Now that he'd mentioned the village, she recalled hearing talk of it during her visits at the market. That's where all their fresh fruits and vegetables always came from, but she'd never strayed close to their lands. She felt content just purchasing their goods from the market and spending her time with her books or her sewing. Of course, like most townsfolk, she kept her own tiny herb garden out in her back yard. It didn't require much care, and it saved her coin by maintaining that herself.

They traveled several more hours, keeping their conversation light between Crystal's chants. Each time she spoke the spell, the pocket watch would tug westward. As the sun cut a path across the sky, she and Logan became confident they'd make it to the farming village before nightfall, even deciding to continue that way if the watch decided to pull another direction; they could set out from the village at the break of dawn and continue their search then. A good night's rest after a hard day's travel sounded too good to pass up, and Logan assured her there would be a small tavern for passersby to spend the night with a hearty meal as an added bonus.

After pocketing the watch and spell, they picked up their pace, wanting to get to Daxonville before the sun fell from view, and by its position in the sky, they only had about an hour left of daylight.

Darkness had fallen by the time they reached the village,

and Crystal followed closely behind Logan as he led the way through the small dusty streets toward where he knew the tavern was located.

As they dismounted their horses, a thin man, with a tweed sun hat, scruffy facial hair, and a stem of grass hanging from his mouth, ambled toward them with his hand out, as if he were reaching for the reins. Crystal pulled Dawn's from his reach, but then Logan took them from her with a smile before passing them over to the man.

"I'll take care of them for yas. Just holler for Jimmy when yas wanna head back out," the man, Jimmy, said before pulling the grass from his lips and spitting. He walked away, guiding the horses behind him as he continued chewing the yellowed grass hanging from his mouth again.

Logan reached for Crystal's hand, and then he led her up the steps and through the swinging doors of the tavern. Once they stepped foot inside, his arm snaked around her waist and tugged her closer.

People filled the room, their garments dusty and grimy from their day's work in the fields. This being the only tavern nearby, the majority of the villagers seemed to come here for a drink after their work, and from the looks of the place, this was a well-knit village. They'd be wise not to step on any toes for the duration of their stay.

They crossed the bar, her nestled within the crook of his arm, and stopped at the counter, where a plump woman stood drying a clear ale mug with a crinkled rag that looked as if it had seen better days. Her brown-eyed gaze snapped up as they approached, and she seemed almost startled to find two patrons she didn't recognize standing before her. She cleared phlegm from her throat, coughing into her hand and wiping it on her apron; Crystal averted her gaze, not wanting to see what was left behind.

"Can I help ya?" she questioned, her voice rough.

Logan dropped coins on the counter. "We'd like a room, and for dinner to be sent up."

The woman flung her rag over her shoulder and put the *cleaned* mug back on the shelf of glassware along the back wall. Then she gathered the coins from the counter, stealing them from view as she pocketed them. She glanced over her shoulder, through a swinging door leading into the kitchens, and yelled, "Gavin!"

A young boy, around the age of sixteen, scurried from the kitchen and stopped at her side. His skin had been darkened by the sun's rays, and his dark hair was closely cropped to his scalp. His gaze lifted to the woman's. "Yes, ma'am?"

"Lead these two up to room three, would ya?" she said to him, pointing to the wall of keys. Then she turned her attention back to Logan and Crystal. "The boy's not too intelligent..." She tapped the side of her head for emphasis. "...but he'll get yous to your room just fine."

"Thank you for your hospitality," Logan replied, his hold on Crystal tightening, as if in warning for her to keep quiet.

She simply nodded her agreement in reply, taking his hint

and keeping her mouth shut.

Gavin hurried from behind the bar once he had their room key in hand, and as he led the way from the main room, Crystal had to stifle a gasp, pressing her lips into a thin line and biting her tongue to keep quiet. Sneaking up from beneath the collar of Gavin's t-shirt were angry red welts, as if he'd been whipped recently. Logan's eyes blazed with anger at the sight, but still he held her tighter. A warning. She'd wait until they were alone before speaking up.

They climbed an old, creaky staircase along the back wall of the place, and once they reached the top, they stood at the beginning of a narrow hallway with peeling green paint along the walls. The floor had once been beautiful hardwood oak but had long since shed its shine for scruffs and scratches.

They came to a stop at the second door on the right, and they waited for Gavin to unlock the door with trembling hands. Once he'd swung open the door, he passed the key to Logan and spun around as if hurrying to escape.

Logan's hand gripped the young boy by the shoulder, and as Gavin stared up with wide eyes full of fright, Crystal's heart nearly split in two as Logan dropped several coins into the boy's pocket. Gavin began shaking his head, his lip shaking as he tried to grab for the coins to return them.

"I-I can't!" he cried, but Logan wouldn't listen.

"You can and you will. Hide them away, bury them if you have to. You will one day escape from beneath her thumb." Logan fixed Gavin with a knowing stare, and Gavin simply nodded.

"Thank you, sir," he said, and then he rushed from the room and out of sight.

As soon as the door closed behind the boy, Crystal turned to Logan. She lifted an arm, waving at the closed door. "What the hell was that about?"

Logan shrugged out of his jacket, hanging the leather over the back of a small wooden chair nestled in the corner. Then he made his way to her side, holding her by her arms as he guided her to the bedside and sitting her down while taking a seat next to her. A nerve twitched in his jaw as he thought of what to say. Finally, he sighed and turned to her.

"I was that kid when I was his age. I found my way to the back of a tavern; the trash bins were a good source of nourishment when I had nothing. A *kind* inn owner took me under their wing, but it wasn't a kindness, not really. That kid is more trapped now than when he was homeless," Logan said, his gaze dropping to his lap as his own memories hung over his thoughts.

She wrapped her hands around his bicep, pulling him into her slightly. His gaze never lifted. "Logan, I didn't know that's how you had spent your childhood. What you did for that boy, I'm sure he'll never forget it. You're a good man, Logan. Never doubt that."

He swung his head around, slowly lifting his chin to look into her eyes. A grin tugged at his lips as he brushed her dark hair back behind her ears. She'd worn it loose today, letting it fall in soft waves down her back. The gentle breeze of the day had been enough to keep her cool.

He gave her a quick peck on the lips. She wanted to deepen the kiss, but then a knock on the door sounded.

Logan stood and answered the door. Gavin rushed in with a tray full of food, and a pitcher of ice water. He set it down on the small rounded table in the corner, and then he quickly left without so much as a single word. Logan's head hung slightly before he motioned toward their dinner.

Crystal joined him at the table to enjoy the meal of mystery meat stew and crusty bread. She could tell that Gavin's presence at the inn still affected Logan, but she didn't know how to help him through it, so she held her tongue.

With their evening meal finished, Crystal emptied her pockets. Seeing the pocket watch and spell again made her curious. She lifted a brow at Logan, the watch dangling from the chain held in her fist. "Should I?"

"I don't see why not," he said, walking around her and dropping his chin to her shoulder as he wrapped his arms around her middle.

She chanted the words she now knew by heart, and then she waited for the chain to tug. The metal grew hotter within her hold, something that hadn't happened during their entire journey thus far, and she gasped as it slowly swung in a tiny circle, over and over and over again.

She glanced sideways to where Logan was still nestled in her neck and fixed him with a stare. "Does that mean..." she began.

"...that he's here?" he finished.

The chain grew too hot to hold, and she dropped the watch to the floor with a clatter. She held onto Logan, her heart racing in her chest. She twisted in his arms until she faced him, her wide gaze latched onto his. Taking a deep breath, she let it out with a whoosh.

"I think Brent is in this village," she said.

He dropped his head to her forehead. "We will find him tomorrow, and then we can end all of this and begin our lives together."

CHAPTER TWELVE

THE MOMENT OF FINDING

THE NEXT MORNING, THEY ATE THEIR BREAKFAST meal down in the tavern; a meal of scrambled eggs, toast, beans, and strips of bacon, all served with coffee and orange juice. Logan had warned her not to ask the locals if they'd seen Brent outright. Without knowing what had happened to him, it was better not to let the villagers know they were searching for someone; these small communities were often a tight-knit group of people, and they'd be wise not to raise their suspicions.

Once they finished their meal, they let the innkeeper know they'd hold the room for the day, and Logan dropped even more coins onto the counter for the woman's greedy hands. She nodded her approval, hiding the coins away in the pockets of her apron and scurrying away with her dirty rag to busy herself with some task or another.

Logan steered Crystal from the tavern with his arm wrapped around her waist, keeping her close anytime anyone was nearby. He was either being protective, or he really didn't trust these folks, and Crystal wasn't sure she wanted the clarification of which way he felt.

The sun's rays filtered through the small cloud covering above, leaving the air around them warm but not stifling. The breeze was cool, and Crystal could feel winter approaching slowly through the chill. They walked leisurely through the dirt paths, taking in the sights around them. There were a few shops in the village, but the land seemed flat and spread out as far as the eye could see.

The dirt paths led from the small village square to lengthy driveways large enough for horses, wagons, and farming equipment to travel, with each path leading to a plot of land with ramshackle wooden buildings dotting the land precariously.

"If you don't want us to ask about for him, how do you propose we find him? The pocket watch doesn't seem to want to guide us any closer," Crystal said, her voice hushed enough for only him to hear.

"Excuse me, sir. My new wife and I are looking to settle

down in the area. You wouldn't happen to have any work I could help with to get us situated, would you?" Logan said to no one, tugging her closer to his side for emphasis.

Crystal gave him a deadpan look before she laughed. Her laughter made him smile as they meandered through the village square.

They checked the shops one-by-one, finding no evidence of Brent. Logan began to lead the way down one of the lengthy driveways toward a farm, and as the time passed with each step they took, Crystal couldn't help but feel her hopes begin to fade. Last night she had been certain today would be the day they found Brent. Knowing he was nearby had her confident it was possible. But there were still too many unknowns.

Why hadn't he returned to her if he was just this short of a distance away from her? It had only taken her and Logan a day's ride to find this village. Was he being held against his will? That realization became more and more plausible the longer they searched, and if that was the case, she doubted even knocking on these farmers' doors would help them locate him any sooner.

She began to fret that finding Brent wouldn't be as easy as she originally thought it would be, and she laughed at that thought because she realized she believed the necromancy part of their quest easier than the searching for Brent part was turning out to be.

The first driveway they traversed took them nearly twenty

minutes of walking to reach the front steps of the house situated on the land. When they arrived and knocked on the door, the woman of the house directed them across the field to the barn with a wave of her hand, pointing the direction to them before closing herself back into her home, which made Crystal's stomach rumble as the scent of fresh baked bread wafted past the threshold before the door shut.

They followed her directions, searching the man of the land out and, upon finding him, Logan immediately went into his speech, asking if the man needed any help keeping up the farm. The man turned Logan down, saying he had hands that worked when he needed them, and apologized as he waved them away.

"When we get back to town, why don't we grab our mounts?" Crystal asked between breaths.

It had been a while since she'd walked this distance, and while the sun wasn't as hot as it had been even a week ago, it still sent rivulets of sweat dripping down her spine and dotting across her brow with the effort of their trek.

"Too bad we didn't have that brilliant plan before now," Logan said, nudging her with his shoulder.

She laughed, nudging him back. He lifted a brow and she squealed, running down the dirt path back toward the village square. He chased her several yards before they both slowed to a walk, laughing as they caught their breath. The mood between them light and free, as if they knew they'd be starting their lives together and escaping Brent's shadow soon.

Once they retrieved their mounts, the search would take less time... if Brent wasn't being held against his will, which she couldn't understand why he wouldn't return to her if that was the case.

She knew she'd always wonder if she didn't find him; knew she'd never be able to close this chapter of her life and start the next one with Logan. And while her love for Logan had grown over the past several weeks, her heart still held Brent close. He'd been the first real love of her life, and he'd always have a place in her heart.

As they made it back to the village square, they stopped and stood watching the villagers carry on their daily tasks around them. Crystal remembered the grungy man from the night prior, who had simply asked them to give a holler should they require his assistance. Was he really within shouting distance of the inn?

"JIMMY!" Logan yelled, grimacing as the passersby glared at him. "Sorry," he mumbled, his clear blue gaze sweeping their surroundings for any sign of Jimmy.

"There!" Crystal pointed.

From between two shops near the inn, just down the road a piece from where they stood, Jimmy's dirty blond hair could be spotted as he poked his head out to see who'd called his name. He still chewed a stalk of long grass, and upon seeing them, he held up a scrawny finger and disappeared around the side of the building again.

A few moments later, Jimmy came down a side street closer to where they waited, holding the reins to both of their mounts as they trailed along behind him. He handed the reins over once Logan dropped a few coins into his outstretched palm, and then he tipped his hat in a farewell and left them to their business.

They walked their horses to the edge of the village, and Crystal pointed to the land next to the farm they'd already checked. Logan nodded as he climbed atop Dusk, and Crystal quickly followed suit.

With their horses, making it to the next house took hardly any time at all. They dismounted, wrapping the reins of their mounts around a low hanging tree limb before making their way toward the front door together.

They climbed the steps and Crystal rapped three times before stepping back, leaving enough room for the screen door to be opened.

A short, stalky woman answered the door, a large white apron draped across her form and a wooden spoon covered in some brown gravy sauce gripped within her pudgy fingers.

"Yes?" she asked from behind the screen door, a cross look between her eyes.

"I was wondering if there might be any work around here you needed help with? My wife and I," Logan said, pulling Crystal into his side, "are thinking of settling down around these parts. I'm looking for work to get us started."

The woman scowled, then she hollered over her shoulder,

"William!"

A tall man, wearing dirt-covered jean overalls and a plaid long-sleeved shirt, stomped through the house until he came into Crystal's view behind the woman. He grumbled and moaned as he made his way to them, and when he stopped just behind the woman's shoulder, he asked, "What's the meaning of this? I was enjoying my late morning tea."

The woman smacked the spoon into her other hand, then waved it at Crystal and Logan. "These folks are new to the area, and they want to settle down in these parts. He's lookin' for a job, he is."

William moved the woman aside and stepped closer to the door. He put a meaty fist on the screen and shoved it open. He gave Logan a look over, his eyes scanning him from his booted feet to his shoulders and head. "You ever do any laborious work before, son?"

"I served in the king's army most of my life, but now I want to settle down with my woman," Logan replied, holding the man's gaze.

"Humph. All right. I'll take a chance on ya. You show up here at the crack of dawn, boy, and I mean the crack of dawn. You better meet me on my fields before the damn roosters start their calling, you hear me?"

"Yes, sir!" Logan replied, nodding.

"Good. Now scrat. I've tea to drink. We start tomorrow!" William grunted as he closed the door, slamming the inside door shut as well.

Logan and Crystal made their way off the front stoop, but by the time they collected their horses, their laughter consumed them. Crystal sat hunched over atop Dawn as she clutched at her stomach, giggling. Logan guffawed while he shook his head, disbelievingly.

Once they'd traveled far enough away, Crystal teased him. "Your plan is working wonders, farmer Joe!"

"Sure, sure. You're all jokes now, but just wait until I come home with that sexy farmer's tan," Logan replied, making Crystal keel over with more giggles.

They tried the same stunt at five more farms, and by the time they were heading to the sixth, Logan had entirely too much work on his hands for the morning. If they didn't soon find Brent, they'd have to leave the village empty handed, or they'd risk being run out of town by the mob of villagers with angry pitchforks waving in the air. Crystal wanted to avoid that if at all possible, though she did have a handy necromancy spell available...

As they stood at the door of the next farm, Logan knocked. They only waited a few moments before footsteps approached them from the other side of the closed door. When the door opened, Crystal gasped, her hands flying to cover her mouth as she took a step back. Logan looked between Crystal and the man at the door, confusion filling his gaze as his brow creased. He placed a hand on her upper arm, giving a gentle squeeze and bringing her attention back to him. She dropped her hands then and stepped closer to Logan's side.

"Crystal?" the man said, pushing the screen door open and stepping out into the evening. "Is that you?"

"Is this?" Logan asked. "Is it him?"

His gaze swung from the man standing in front of him to Crystal, waiting for an answer.

"No," she replied. "It's Thomas; Brent's brother."

Thomas invited them into his home, where they sat around a low-burning fireplace while they sipped his homemade brew of ale. As the sun began to fall from its place in the sky and night raced to take its place, he offered them a room in his home, which they humbly accepted. Once the small talk had passed, and the silence became awkward, Crystal told Thomas why they were really there.

"As you know, your brother and I were waiting to begin our lives together until the wars had finished. I waited and waited, but he never returned. Eventually, I found Logan, and together, after we received the news of his survival, we set out in search of him.

"I couldn't move on with my life without first knowing if he was okay," she explained, leaving all their dark magic out of it. It had become a taboo topic since the king's hunt on the dark sorcerers.

"He never returned to you?" Thomas asked.

"No, he didn't. At first, I was terribly worried he'd suffered a terrible fate fighting the king's war, but when I found that not to be the case, I began searching. I was given a spell of finding that led me here, so I'm certain he is nearby."

Thomas cocked a brow. "A spell led you here?"

She drew the pocket watch from her pocket, wishing she'd had the good grace to clean it before having to present it to someone.

A muscle ticked in Thomas' jaw, and Crystal made a mental note to wipe the blood away at her earliest convenience. He reached a hand out and plucked the watch from her grasp.

"Where did you get this?" Thomas asked.

"Your brother gave it to me as a parting gift."

"It wasn't his to give. It is mine."

"Then he isn't near here, is he?" Crystal asked, her voice deflating with her hope.

"No, he isn't. Last I had heard from him, he was heading to start his life in the northern hills of Dargonia. I had assumed he would be with you," Thomas said.

"I reside in the southern hills," Crystal said.

She put her half-drank mug of ale down on the table in front of them and stood. "I'm sorry to take up so much of your time, Thomas. I think it's best if Logan and I leave now."

"I thought you wanted to stay the night?"

"It was a kind offer, but we have the night paid out for us at the inn."

Logan climbed to his feet, placing his empty mug next to Crystal's on the table. "Thank you for your hospitality, but I think we'd like to get our things in order to set out at first light. I know Crystal will feel better knowing how your brother fares sooner rather than later."

"You're a good man to look after another man's woman like this," Thomas said, but Crystal didn't miss the underlying tone of accusation.

"Yes, he is," Crystal replied in a rush, her fingers gripping Logan's as they made their way to the front door; Thomas followed them to show them out.

Darkness had fallen while they'd sat inside, but the sky was clear enough that the light of the moon would be enough to guide them back to the inn within the village square. They donned their jackets and stepped out into the night, bidding Thomas farewell and leaving his farm behind them.

Nearly thirty minutes later, they dismounted outside the tavern, where Jimmy rushed out of the shadows and guided their mounts away without a word. The way he kept doing that unnerved Crystal, and she was glad they'd be leaving this place behind in the morning.

It would seem tomorrow would be the start of yet another journey.

It took Crystal and Logan three days to make it to the bottom of the mountains just north of Dargonia. The path through the mountains would be a strenuous one, and so they stabled their horses at the bottom and searched the single shop near the start of the trail upward for better gear that would help them climb the trickier parts.

Logan asked the shopkeeper if there were any locals who made their homes on the hills above, and the shopkeeper informed them of a single, small village half-a-day's trek up the mountain's path, though he warned them of how much they prized their privacy.

The path through the mountains was tiring, and as they pushed themselves forward, they remained silent, focusing instead on the task at hand. They encountered no issues, save for the steep areas that slowed their progress to a snail's pace, and just as the shopkeeper had said, they came to the outskirts of a small village within a matter of hours.

The first thing they noticed were the tall gates surrounding each home. The shopkeeper wasn't kidding when he'd mentioned their love of privacy.

"So? What's the plan?" Crystal asked, pulling her jacket closed tighter around her trembling frame. The snow-capped mountains above seemed to be sharing their frost with the village below, and the temperature had dropped several degrees during their climb. Now that they had stopped moving, the chill bit through her jacket and stole her warmth.

"I doubt the whole farm-hand thing will work up here. Should we just go for the truth?"

She swept her gaze across the handful of houses before them. Shrugging, she replied, "Why not? They're predisposed to hate us already, aren't they?"

He chuckled. "I suppose they are."

They made it to the first door within a matter of minutes, and as Logan knocked on the front door, Crystal held her hands over her ears; the chill becoming almost too much for her to bear. They'd need to find their way to warmth soon, or head back down the mountain to escape the brutal cold.

A man answered the door, glaring down at the open gate behind them before letting his gaze fall to them. "What can I do for you?" he asked, none too kindly.

"We're searching for a man named Brent. We have news from his family," Logan replied.

"Brent? Yeah, he lives in the blue house over there," the man answered, pointing to a house across the way a piece.

"Thank you, sir," Logan said, bowing his head slightly in thanks.

"Sure. Close the gate on your way out." The door slammed shut as they turned to head in the direction the man had pointed.

Once they'd made it back to the main path, and closed the

gate behind them, they walked toward the blue house just a few homes down from the first place they'd stopped.

Crystal felt almost giddy, knowing their trail ended soon and they would be able to put all this uneasiness behind them. She didn't feel she could move forward with Logan until she'd closed the door between her and Brent, and she wanted to make sure he was at least okay before she started her life with Logan. She owed him that much given how much they had loved each other during his visits, and during the time before he had been sent away to fight the king's war against the dark sorcerers.

"Well, that was easier than I thought it would be," she said as they neared the blue home.

Logan smiled down at her. "It's about time you found some snippet of good luck," he joked. "Every turn you've taken seemed to have led you to an entire new maze to traverse. Finally, you'll reach the end of this quest."

"It hasn't *all* been bad luck..."

He looked at her and winked. "Oh, honey, I know."

"You know, in your analogy you just shared, you're the cheese," she said, watching him with a straight face until he laughed.

She was still laughing as they approached the front door of the blue house. She knocked on the door and stepped back, suddenly nervous.

A moment later and the door swung open, revealing Brent. Crystal's eyes widened just as Brent's did, and a slow smile stretched across her lips at having found her missing lover. She took a step forward, wanting to close the distance between them but stopping when a voice called from behind him.

"Brent, baby? Who is it?" a feminine voice cooed from somewhere upstairs.

A scowl fell across Crystal's face and she clenched her fists. The woman came into view as she descended the stairs wearing only a thin nightgown, as if they'd stayed in bed all day long. Her angry gaze flicked between Brent and the woman, and Logan's fingers closed around her tensed hand.

Logan pulled her into his side, wrapping his arm around her waist and keeping her close.

The woman came to stand next to Brent, folding her dainty hands over his shoulder and leaning into him. She kissed his cheek before turning her attention on their guests.

"Who are these people, baby?" she asked, her voice soft as a bunny's arse.

Crystal saw only red when Brent replied with a shrug. "I haven't the faintest clue, honey. Why don't you wait upstairs for me and I'll see what they want?"

CHAPTER THIRTEEN

THE UNLEASHED RAGE

CRYSTAL SHOVED BRENT BACKWARD WITH enough force he lost his balance and fell to the floor. The half-naked woman backed away until she hit the wall next to the stairway leading to the second floor. Crystal paid her no mind, her focus on Brent sprawled on the floor before her.

She stormed toward him, Logan remaining where he stood at the door, watching silently. Crystal waved a hand at him, her rage spilling from her lips in a growling rush.

"I thought you were dead! You have no idea what I've been through! What I've done to try to *rescue* you!" Her words fell from her like poisonous venom from the fangs of a snake.

Brent raised himself up onto his elbows, watching as Crystal approached with her fist shaking angrily above him as she yelled out her frustrations. His gaze flicked to where the woman stood, inching toward the bottom step.

Digging her fist into her pocket, Crystal pulled a crumpled ball of a page from where she'd hidden the spell. She didn't think she'd ever find a need for it, but the spell was too easy to cast to risk it falling into someone else's clutches. She began unfolding the paper, straightening it as she stood over Brent. She pointed a finger at the woman, not even bothering to glance her way.

"Make her stop moving *right* now, if you know what's best," Crystal threatened, her jaw tight with each word.

Brent nodded. "Listen to her."

"Baby, who is this?" the woman asked again, fear shaking her voice as she spoke.

"Yea, *baby.* Why don't you tell her who I am?" Crystal mocked the woman, folding her arms across her chest as she finally glanced her way.

Her hair fell down her back and in front of her shoulders in soft waves of light blond, her big doe eyes so wide the whites stretched around the brown irises, and her pale skin the shade of fright, as if she'd spotted a ghost... or something worse. She was pretty, Crystal could see that much, but she looked nothing like Crystal, whom Brent had supposedly loved and promised his return.

"Do we seriously have to do this?" Brent asked, lifting a brow as he gazed over her shoulder to where she knew Logan still stood. "It's not as if you've arrived alone..."

Fury furrowed her brow and she practically snarled at him. She smacked her palm across her chest, screeching at him, "Me? You want to lump me into the same jack-assery pile as you?" She shook her head as she glanced down at the page still clutched within her hold. "Tell her who I am, Brent. Now!"

Shame fell across his features, his body sagging as he looked at his whore from beneath a hooded gaze. He clenched his jaw, clearly angry at the situation in which his actions had placed him. Crystal watched him grimace before he revealed the truth, which everyone within the room knew, except the blonde bimbo.

"This is Crystal. She was my lover before I joined the king's army," Brent said, his voice almost too-quiet to placate Crystal.

"You said you weren't involved when we met," the woman replied, her brows pulling together as she glared across the room at where he still sat at Crystal's feet. "You lied to me?"

"I didn't think she'd wait. I thought she'd forget about me. I figured she'd meet someone new," Brent explained, his sapphire gaze flicking to Logan again.

Crystal figured Brent wondered why Logan was involved in this at all. Why he stood silently, just watching. From the looks of things, the two of them hadn't known each other in the army, that much was clear.

She didn't know what Logan was thinking, but as she glanced over her shoulder at him, he stood tall, his face blank as he winked at her. He would do what she wanted. She should have known he'd be okay with her actions, regardless of where they might lead. If he was okay with raising the dead, then he would be okay with her angry outburst. Logan felt he owed her a life-debt, something she'd spend the rest of her life trying to shake from him. He didn't owe her anything. In fact, he'd already given her too much. He made her realize she was worth more than she ever thought she was; he made her confident, and brave.

"You just left her waiting?" the woman asked. The tone the woman used made Crystal glance her way. When she regarded her, she found a pity flaring to life behind her downcast brown eyes.

Brent's head dropped, his chin resting against his chest as his shoulders sagged even more.

When the woman gasped, she brought her hands to her mouth as she stared in horror at the man she'd thought she'd known. She looked to Crystal, dropping her hands to her side. "I'm so sorry. That must have been awful."

A little of Crystal's anger dissipated, and she pointed toward the stairs. "I will leave you out of my revenge, but you need to stay upstairs."

She watched the woman carefully, wanting to see if any hint

of defiance flickered beneath her saddened gaze. When she saw no sign of trouble, she turned away as the woman scurried up the stairs, disappearing somewhere on the second floor and leaving her alone to enact her vengeance on the man who had put her through hell.

She had worried for his well-being for months while he fought the king's war. She'd traveled to town weekly in search of any news at all. When she'd finally found the army returned, she dreaded having to go through the sick house, but she'd done that too for what she'd believed to be her true love. And when she'd found no answers there, she'd assumed him dead and had mourned that loss.

Meanwhile, he'd been here this entire time, screwing some blonde she couldn't even bring herself to hate any longer.

Stepping forward, her eyes flicked to the page in her grip. She smiled, a slow, malicious grin that had Brent backing away from her in a crawl. She shook her empty hand at him, pointing her finger as if she were scolding a five-year-old.

"I waited for you for far too long. I know exactly what I plan to do to you now," Crystal said, keeping her speech slow and steady while trying to inflict fear just with her low tone of voice. She wanted him afraid. She wanted him to worry. She wanted to inflict as many horrible emotions onto him as possible after everything he had put her through.

"This isn't you, Crys," Brent said, his hands lifting before him in some weak defense that would do him no good. He glanced toward the doorway again, not able to forget Logan's presence.

"You have no idea who I am now, Brent. No idea what I've been through or what I've done in my search to find you. And you can stop looking to him for help; he's perfectly content letting me have my revenge." She turned her head sideways, aiming her next words over her shoulder. "Isn't that right, Logan?"

She listened to his footsteps approaching, her grin stretching further. He stood just behind her right shoulder, his hand giving it a gentle squeeze as he said, "Of course it is, my love."

Brent's eyes widened at the term of endearment, his eyes flicking between the two of them as he crawled backward another pace. The back of his head connected with the wall, though not hard enough to cause him pain; just enough to send his fear racing through his veins now that he knew he'd been cornered.

"Do you have any last words?" Crystal asked.

"What?" Brent exclaimed. "No, you can't!"

"What a waste," Logan said, shaking his head as he dropped his hold of Crystal's shoulder. "A request for forgiveness, a message for a loved one, or hell, even some vindictive retort would all have been better options for your last words."

Smiling, Crystal began to chant.

"Wicked hearts and sinful desires,

Revenge is what this one requires.
Fierce souls and mighty retribution,
These last words bring your execution."

She shoved the paper back into her pocket and watched him. The spell hadn't listed how long it would take before it took effect, but she couldn't imagine it taking too long. The room fell so quiet as they waited, Crystal figured someone would be able to hear a pin drop onto a carpet of cotton balls. After a few moments, Brent's lips lifted into a slow grin.

"Looks like those won't be my last words after all," Brent said.

His confidence didn't last long though. His eyes widened, lifting into his skull until only the bottoms of his sapphire irises could be seen. Bringing his hands up, he gripped at his throat as if he could no longer breathe, his mouth opening and closing like a lazy fish swimming in a glass bowl. The color of his lips turned a shade of bluish-green while his skin paled to a sickly shade of white. When he started spewing white foam from his mouth, Crystal took a step back, colliding into Logan.

Logan wrapped his arms around her middle as he set his chin to her shoulder, pulling them back from the scene before them as blood began spilling from every orifice of Brent's. The bloody tears streamed down his face and tinted the foam falling from his lips a pinkish hue that almost made Crystal gag.

She turned from him then, hiding her face in Logan's

179

shoulder as she twisted in his hold. When he held her tighter, she sighed. It was as if a weight had been lifted now that her revenge had been enacted.

They stood like that, holding onto each other while they listened to the death sounds escaping Brent's crumpled form. It wasn't exactly the most romantic moment of her life, but she couldn't help but admire Logan's love for her. She didn't know how many couples could do what they'd just done together and come out the other side still holding onto one another in a loving embrace.

It took several moments for Brent to quiet behind her, and when he did, Logan filled the silence with a question.

"What do you want to do now?"

She took a step back from him, her hands falling to her sides. Slipping her fingers into her pockets, she felt the crinkled paper of the spells the old hag had given to her. An idea formed in her mind and she glanced up at Logan, a smile tugging at her lips.

"He made me wait for so long. How about we make him wait too?"

Logan lifted a brow, not understanding what she intended. She pulled the spells from her pocket and showed him the grave dirt necromancy spell. His eyes widened as he figured out her meaning, then he nodded, grinning.

"We should probably do this here," he said, making his way to Brent's corpse.

When Crystal nodded, he bent down to retrieve the body. Crystal hurried in front of him, leading the way through the house until she found what she was looking for: a back door. She opened it a crack, peering out into the back yard and shoving the door open further when she noticed the tall privacy fence surrounding the property. They had a hot tub back here, which most likely explained the height of the fence they'd used; a factor that would make her intentions easier to pull off unhindered.

"Maybe you should wait inside while I bury him in a shallow grave," Logan suggested, his gaze lifting over his shoulder to the second floor of the house.

She followed his eyes and scowled as she noticed the curtains swaying, as if someone had been watching from above. She nodded, turning back toward the house and leaving Logan to carry out the heavy lifting on his own.

If it weren't for the blonde upstairs, she'd have provided whatever aid she could to the task at hand, but she didn't want to risk the woman racing out to a neighbor seeking help. Not that they'd arrive in time to do anything now...

Though . . . they could prevent her from enacting her final plan for vengeance, but she wouldn't let it come to that.

She pulled one of Brent's living room chairs to the hallway, angling it so she had a clear view of the stairs leading up, as well as the hallway Logan would enter when he'd finished burying Brent's corpse.

Sitting, she waited until it was time to raise the dead.

CHAPTER FOURTEEN

THE REVENGE OF A NECROMANCER

AN HOUR LATER, LOGAN CAME INSIDE COVERED in dirt and sweat. Long rivulets of grimy perspiration streaked down his face, and he wiped it away with the back of his hand, which only made his face dirtier. He'd lost his shirt and jacket, despite the chilly air at this height of altitude halfway up the northern mountains; the exertion of digging a shallow grave enough to keep him warm as his heart pumped his blood quicker with his effort.

He walked toward her without taking his muddy boots off, leaving a trail of dirt clumps littering the floor in his wake. She waited until he stopped before her, and then she rose to wrap her arms around his neck, pulling him in for a kiss.

At first, he tried to shrug away from her hold, probably assuming himself too dirty to touch, but as her lips connected with his, all fight left his shoulders as he bent down and scooped her up into his arms.

As they pulled free of the kiss, he set her back down on her toes, stepping back while keeping his hold on her hips. He flicked a gaze up the flight of stairs, lifting a brow before asking, "Did she give you any trouble?"

"No," Crystal replied, "I haven't heard a sound."

She glanced over his shoulder to where he'd come from, pursing her lips with her own inquiry at the tip of her tongue. "Is the deed done?"

Logan nodded. "It's a shallow grave, but it should do the trick." He dropped his forehead to hers, breathing in her scent and fixing her with a serious look. "Are you sure about this?"

She chewed her lip while she thought about what they were about to do. Seeing him lying there, dead against the wall, she'd felt so sure of what she'd wanted. Now? Could she really be sure? She knew she'd be okay living her life with Logan, more than okay. They had their book shop in town, and honestly, it provided a better income than the little bit of needlework she used to do for the townsfolk.

She fixed him with a stare, imagining their perfect lives together. Spending their days working the shop, their evenings at their home in the hills.

"He could come in handy. From what I can remember, he was a pretty good cook. Imagine, waking up to breakfast, coming home to dinner, and never having to keep house. We can spend all our time focusing on us and our shop."

Logan grinned, shaking his head slightly. "It would be nice..."

"Besides, whenever we get sick of him, we can just bury him again..." Crystal laughed.

She unlatched her arms from around his neck and they made their way to the back door together. Crystal made a quick stop in the kitchen for the only ingredient they would require aside from Brent's fresh grave dirt; salt. With a small burlap sack of salt in her hand, she followed Logan out the door, down the back-porch steps, and to the foot of where he'd buried Brent's corpse.

Their backyard was a fair size, with a hot tub off to the left of where Logan had dug the shallow grave and the back of the fence several yards out from where they currently stood. There was a large tree nestled into the back corner of the yard, with a romantic wooden swing hanging from the lowest weight-bearing branch. A garden of flowers strong enough to grow in a chillier climate sat not far off, painting the perfect atmosphere for a couple to enjoy one another.

This wasn't a romantic scene though. Not as they stood over Brent's grave. Crystal held onto the spell within the grip of one hand, and a bag of salt still clutched in her other.

Logan had walked around the grave, standing across from where Crystal stood and waiting for her to begin.

She took a deep breath, tilted her head to the sky, and watched the falling sun for a moment, trying to will herself the courage to perform the ritual.

A symbol coated the bottom half of the page, with instructions for her to place that symbol, in salt, on the ground around the grave of the one she wished to raise. She opened the brown sack, just enough to pour a small stream of salt, and she bent forward, walking slowly around the grave as she poured the white powder circle and five-pointed star from the example under the spell.

She threw the empty salt bag over her shoulder, opened the spell, and looked across the circle to where Logan stood.

He gave a nod, his eyes drifting to the ground beneath their feet. She followed his gaze and noticed grains of salt already drifting away in the slight breeze.

They'd have to make this quick, but as far as she could tell, it was as simple as reading the spell off the sheet with Brent's grave dirt clutched in her fist. Speaking of which, she bent down and grabbed as much dirt as she could fit into her tiny hold. She straightened, cleared her throat, and began to read from the sheet held within her other hand.

"This grave belongs to the dead,
The life within taken too soon,

Their fullest life was not led,

Please, Gatekeeper, grant us this boon.

With the power within to open the gates,

Grant this dead with life once more,

Change what's been written by the fates,

This corpse's life you must restore!"

Crystal gasped when the wound on her thumb, which had healed days ago, split open again. The pain of the flesh tearing apart caused her to drop her hold on the dirt, and Brent's grave dirt fell back to the ground coated in her blood as her wound dripped crimson. The blood price had been paid, even if that hadn't been included in this spell; it seemed it took what it needed regardless. She rubbed the wound on her hip and watched for any sign that the spell had worked.

When the last words had fallen from her lips, rumbling sounded from somewhere above as the sun set further and darkened the land quicker than what felt normal. She took a step back, not wanting to stand so close to the fresh grave as the light faded from the yard and the shadows stretched eerily closer.

The hag's words played in her mind about how raising the dead was an act better suited for the shadows, and Crystal shivered.

According to the page she still held, whoever cast the spell of raising would hold complete control over the one raised. She had nothing to fear of Brent now, and yet her body trembled. She blamed the cold of course, but as she gripped her arms around her middle, her emerald eyes glued to the clumps of dirt in front of her, she knew it wasn't just the cold causing her to shake. Lifting her gaze, she pierced Logan with a worried glance, chewing her lip as they waited. The night around them too quiet to calm her nerves.

Crystal gasped as the dirt at her feet began to rumble, shaking loose dirt from the piles as Brent awoke buried beneath two feet of ground. She watched with wide eyes as his fingers inched above the grave, stretching as he shoved more of his arm further into the air. Shaking her head, she silently chastised herself for being afraid or shocked. What the hell did she expect would happen? She performed a spell of necromancy for the love of...

Brent's arm shot out of the grave, bending at the elbow as his fingers began to claw at the dirt. His other arm pulled free, shoving more clumps of dirt aside as he tried to break free of the earth's hold. The faint sounds of his moaning came from the ground, growing louder as more dirt fell aside.

Taking another step back, Crystal stared across the grave to where Logan currently stood. His face remained blank as he watched the sight before him. When he noticed her looking at him, he gave her a reassuring smile, which put her worries at ease.

The dirt roiled, more of it falling away from the center of

the shallow grave. A moment later, Brent's hair broke through, followed by the rest of his head and shoulders and chest as he sat up slowly within his grave. His eyes remained closed while his hands brushed away the crud from his face. Once he seemed satisfied, his eyes blinked open.

A gasp escaped Crystal at the sight of Brent's eyes, which no longer held the sapphire color she had adored so much when they had been together before. Instead, his pupils seemed larger, the irises almost consumed with the black hue, leaving only a sliver of the deep blue to ring each eye.

With his vision cleared, he brushed away the remaining dirt in a matter of minutes and climbed free of what could very well have been his last resting place... if Crystal hadn't had other plans for him.

He paused. Stopping before Crystal and standing still.

"Brent?" she asked, not sure what to do now. The spell had ended with the casting; it never mentioned what would come next, which was something she should probably have considered before getting this far.

"Yes, Crystal?" he replied, his voice monotonous and not anything like how he used to speak. If anyone who knew him spoke to him now, they'd surely notice the difference too.

"Are you ready to go home?"

His head swept toward the house, and he studied it for a moment before returning his gaze to her. He lifted his brows in question, then raised a hand to gesticulate the door. "Home?"

She shook her head. "Not this home. Our home. Will you help Logan and me get back home?"

At the mention of another name, Brent swung his gaze around the darkened yard until he found Logan, who still stood on the other side of the now-empty grave. He looked back at Crystal, flicking a thumb over his shoulder to indicate Logan. "Logan?"

She nodded.

"Yes. I will help you and Logan home," Brent replied. "How can I help?"

Logan side-stepped around the grave and came to stand next to Crystal. He wrapped an arm around her middle and whispered into her ear, "The woman has been watching us from the upstairs win—Don't look now! Let's just grab a few provisions, take an empty pack-sack, and leave before she can bring any trouble down over our heads."

"Good plan," she said to Logan. To Brent, she asked, "Do you have any empty packs in the house we can use for our trip home?"

Brent nodded and began to lead the way into the house. His joints seemed a bit stiff, and he certainly needed a bath, but other than those two things, he seemed okay. They should probably have him wash a bit before they leave for home, she realized. Otherwise, he'd bring too much unwanted attention their way.

Once they made it back inside the house, Crystal followed

Brent around while asking Logan to go search for some clean clothes for Brent to wear. She didn't think it wise to send Brent upstairs, not when the woman, whoever she may be, was still held like a prisoner within her own home. No, that was a job better suited for Logan. He'd find suitable travel clothes and make sure the woman stayed put until after they'd left.

When Brent pulled out an empty sack from the bottom of a closet filled with jackets, shoes, and other outdoor gear, Crystal immediately went to the kitchen to fill the pack with provisions for their trip home. Dried meats, berries, and some cheese would be more than enough for the short trip back home; it wouldn't take more than three days' travel to make it back to her hills.

Logan came down the stairs with fresh clothes in his arms only minutes later, and they guided their new pet outside into the backyard, motioning to the hot tub. It wasn't necessarily supposed to be used for cleaning yourself, but Crystal thought it best that Brent avoid the upstairs, and the woman they intended to leave behind.

She had to grab him by the shoulder to stop him from climbing into the tub with the cover still on while he was still clothed. While Logan removed the cover and twisted the dial that would release furnace heat from the house into the hot tub, Crystal helped strip Brent of his clothing, leaving only his underwear firmly in place. All lust for the man had perished when she'd fallen for Logan, and if it hadn't by then, it certainly would have upon witnessing his death... and resurrection.

Once he was clean enough to travel without raising any unwanted attention, they slipped out the backyard through the gate next to the house. The dark skies of night provided the perfect cover for their retreat as they hurried through the village and down the mountain path.

It took them most of the night to climb down the somewhat steep incline of the mountain. Each step they took planned carefully to avoid falling to their death. While they now knew how to raise the dead, it was clear from Brent's vacant face that rising from the grave did not come without a price.

By morning, they made it to where they'd left their horses. Crystal and Logan sat atop Dusk, while they gave Brent Dawn to ride; she wasn't as nervous as Dusk, who had began nickering as soon as they approached with the dead-but-not-dead Brent.

Once they'd mounted their steeds, they rode for home, where Crystal and Logan couldn't wait to begin their new lives together.

EPILOGUE

One year later...

"THANK YOU! YOU TOO," CRYSTAL SAID, WISHING the last customer of the day farewell as they skipped out of the shop after having found their next read.

The storm last night had broken thick branches from several of the trees surrounding their property on the hills, and so Logan had stayed home today to help Brent fix up the place while she rode into town to open their shop. Without him by her side on the way into town, and without him here during the day to keep her company during the lulls, she had missed him. There hadn't been many opportunities to do such over the past year, as they'd made sure to spend as much time together as

193

possible.

Crystal hurried to tidy the place up, leaving all the restocking for the morning. She'd have Logan's help then, and she didn't want to waste another moment apart. Once she'd closed the till and flipped the open sign to closed, she grabbed her jacket and locked up, rushing down the streets as the sun began to lose its heat for the evening.

Her horse, Dawn, was right where she had left her, chewing clumps of dirty grass in the pen for travelers. Her and Logan had talked about turning the back yard of the shop into an area for their mounts, but she'd mentioned not believing the space to be large enough for more than one mount at a time.

He had winked at her and she'd laughed, shaking her head and dismissing his often-requested shared mount idea. She loved Logan, she really did, but nothing beat the feel of power received from steering your own mount whichever way you pleased.

Having made this trip almost daily for the past year, Crystal could almost make the ride home with her eyes shut, and if she couldn't, Dawn sure could have. It took nearly two full hours before she crested the top of a hill and her home came into view in one of the valleys.

She could already tell that the men had been busy, most of the debris that had littered their land before she'd left for town had been thrown into a large pile. She'd have to get Brent to take that into the barn; it would make for great kindling when the time came to relight their hearth.

As soon as she came close enough to the house to be noticed, Brent started making his way toward her. She dismounted and he wordlessly took the reins from her, leading her horse to the stables. He'd feed and water Dawn, and he'd even brush her coat until it shined, just as Crystal had trained him to within the first weeks of arriving back home.

It hadn't taken them long to train him, and the more they interacted with him, the more natural his voice sounded. Still, they both regarded him more of a pet than anything else, a very useful around the house kind of pet.

Logan hadn't liked the idea of sharing their home with him though, and Crystal hadn't argued when Logan began to construct a small apartment-sized dwelling in the loft of the barn. With that in place for Brent, he only ever entered their home when they invited him inside, which didn't happen often. He had no reason to eat, so he didn't have to consume their meals. His body didn't require removing its waste, so he didn't need their indoor plumbing. He was like a reanimated corpse, but magic kept him from decaying, a fact for which Crystal's senses were thankful.

With her horse taken care of, she turned toward the house. She stopped in her tracks at the sight of Logan, bare chested and his sweat glistening under the sun's rays. She licked her lips as she made her way toward him.

Once he noticed her, he met her halfway with a smile

stretched across his stubbly face.

"How was business?" he asked, wrapping his arms around her and pulling her close. His lips grazed her cheek in a soft kiss before he pulled back to peer down into her emerald gaze with affection.

She rose up on her tiptoes, not ready to pull away yet, and kissed him quick on the lips. He grinned down at her as she lowered herself and answered him, "Steady as usual. It's really picking up since we started that book club."

"There's always a trick to boost business. You just have to find it." He wrapped an arm around her shoulder and guided her inside, not dropping her gaze as they walked.

"What's for dinner tonight? I'm famished!"

Logan pulled open the door and the scent of grilled boar hit her nose. A small gasp escaped her as she noticed the entryway, and she shirked out of his hold to follow the petals, which thankfully weren't white with black tips.

She didn't know when he'd found the time to do it, but Logan had filled the entryway with burning white candles, while scarlet red rose petals littered the floor in a path to a small table set for two. As she walked past the stairwell, she didn't miss the petals leading somewhere more romantic.

She stopped near the table and spun to face him. A smile lighting her eyes as she giggled. "What's all this for?"

"Do I need a reason?" he asked, leaning casually against the railing leading upstairs as he stared at her; his head tilted to the side as if he was admiring the view, which he probably was, knowing him.

She grinned. "No, I suppose you don't."

Logan started walking toward her, slowly, as if he were a predator and she his prey. Each step sent excitement soaring through her veins. She could feel the heat blooming in her face as she watched him, bare chested as he approached her with a gleam in his eye and a sexy half-grin while he watched her with his head tilted.

"Now," he said, his voice low enough that it sent shivers of delight down her spine. "The only question is: Do you want dinner first... or dessert?"

She licked her lips as he stopped before her. Crystal knew exactly what she wanted first. She walked next to him, looping her arm around his neck as she passed and pulling him after her gently, her fingers trailing along the nape of his sweat-dampened neck as she guided him to the stairs.

Standing on the first step up, she turned to face him, looping her arms around his neck and grinning. Every moment with Logan had filled her heart to capacity with love. She kissed him, parting her lips to breathe him in as she deepened their kiss. When she pulled away, the same passion burning through her veins shone through his hooded, clear blue gaze.

Grabbing his hand and threading her fingers through his, she pulled him up the stairs as if she were back in her teenage years trying to hide away her secret love from her parents. The thought sent thrills through her, and she rushed for their bedroom at the top of the stairs.

It hadn't taken them long to turn the spare room into a home office slash home library, moving Logan into her bed almost as soon as they arrived back home from their journeys. Falling asleep with him next to her, holding her and whispering endearments into her sleepy gaze every night, made her feel like she'd been the one to die and go to heaven. Waking up with him, teasing her as they started their day off on the right foot, made her certain of her heavenly living arrangement.

Crystal backed into her room, already tugging her t-shirt from her back and dropping it on the floor, which she noticed Logan had distributed red and white rose petals along as well. She grabbed the sides of his head, tugging him to her and kissing him as if her very life depended on it as his messy dark brown hair tickled her fingertips. Her fingers splayed down his back, relishing the feel of his glistening skin as she dug her nails into his muscle.

She'd nearly made it to the edge of the bed when Logan shimmied her brown cargo pants down her hips, and she stepped out of them as the back of her knees collided with her mattress. Her eyes widened at the mischievous glint in Logan's eyes as his fingers brushed her shoulders, and laughter erupted form her when he pushed her over the edge, sending her cascading backward until she landed on top of their bed.

The soft touch of petals coated her skin, as Logan had made

sure no surface went without his romantic makeover. Candles flickered on their dresser and bedside tables, casting them both in a seductive glow as the lights and shadows danced upon their naked flesh.

Biting her lip to hold back her squeals of delight as Logan climbed atop her, she scooted further back on the bed until her head hit the pillows, her hair fanning out around her in a messy chestnut halo as Logan covered her body with his own.

He'd lost his trousers, and his underwear, and she didn't remember when he'd stripped, but she certainly admired the feel of his subtle touches as his thigh brushed against hers before he widened his stance above her. Each small touch sent her heart racing for more, and a content sigh fell from her as his lips collided with hers.

He trailed kisses from her lips to her jaw to her neck and eventually to her ear, his scruffy stubble tickling her as his chin cut a path behind each of his tender kisses. She loved how he always seemed to keep just enough facial hair to scratch her soft skin, and she relished the feel of it as his lips trailed lower, and lower still.

He awakened her passion full force as his hand cupped her breast, his fingers teasing the nipple while his mouth sent her sailing toward a release she wanted to keep at bay.

She wasn't ready for this to be over, not so soon, and so she grabbed Logan's head and pulled him from her core, bringing his mouth to hers for a taste before flipping him over so that she could ride him.

With her hair hanging in a curtain around her, she trailed her own kisses down his chest, loving what her mouth could do to him. His skin held the salty taste of a day of hard work, and as she hit the spots that made him wild, she savoured the quick intakes of breath he'd pull in and the soft moans of pleasure filling the room along with the sounds her mouth produced as she pulled his length within.

Within minutes, Logan's hands fisted the sheets. Not being able to take any more of her attentions, he grabbed her by the arms and pulled her up to him, kissing her deeply before he flipped their position somewhat roughly.

Passion filled his clear blue gaze as he stared down at her; his forehead dotted with sweat from their desires and his hair damp and disheveled. He shook his head slightly, his lips tugging into a seductive grin before he spoke.

"I can't wait any longer. It's time for my dessert."

With a mess of soft rose petals filling the room with their splendor and their scent, Logan and Crystal filled the room with the sound of their hard love making. Something both of them would be content doing for the rest of their lives.

It had been their grief that had pulled them to this moment, but as they both rocketed toward their own release, those heart-wrenching days were the last things on their minds.

And unbeknownst to them both, those hard times would be the farthest from their thoughts as life began to bloom within their womb.

ACKNOWLEDGMENTS

A big shout out to the four little people who made this book possible by giving their mommy some quiet every now and then so that she could write this beauty. It really is a family effort, and their patience with me when I'm deep in my writing cave will always be appreciated. Reach for your dreams; the sky really is the limit.

I can't write a book without thanking the rest of the Atomic Indies. Not only do they support me during the months of writing, but they are absolutely lifesaving as release day approaches. Ali Winters, Trish Beninato, Tiki Kos, I don't know where I'd be without you, but, luckily, I don't have to find out. Thanks for always sticking by my side. You hippies are the best.

There are two betas in particular who I have to mention.

Boo Vickery, you already know how much I value your continued support. Thanks for making me always feel like a star. And Alexis Vorpahl, your input helped shape this book into the lovely story it turned into, so thank you. I look forward to working with you both again. I couldn't do this without your support.

And last, but certainly not least, to all the readers who happen to pick a copy of Death's Kiss up. Thank you. I hope you enjoy the read as much as I enjoyed the write. We authors would be nothing without you, and I will forever be grateful to each and every one of you.

Until our next read,

Lexi Swann

Xx

Lexi Swann began her career in the writing world as a freelance editor. After five years polishing authors' manuscripts, she began writing her own stories. She spends her days juggling her large family, working as an attendant to the handicapped, editing, and writing. You can find this adorable Canadian sipping coffee while she plots her next works in a small, blink and you'll miss it, town in Quebec.

www.lexiswann.com

Subscribe:
www.subscribepage.com/LexiSwann